Wuthe...

Heathcliff will never know how much I love him. Whatever our souls are made of, his and mine are the same. He is always, always on my mind.

Wuthering Heights is a love story – but a love story like no other ever written.

Wuthering Heights is a house in the wild, wind-blown north of England. There, Cathy Earnshaw grows up with Heathcliff, a strange boy whom her father found in the dirty streets of Liverpool, starving, homeless and half-dead. Their love for each other grows but, when she is old enough to marry, Cathy chooses the rich Edgar Linton.

And so begins a terrible story of revenge. Heathcliff can never forgive Cathy or Linton and promises never to rest until both their families are destroyed. But there is one thing he cannot kill – his love of Cathy.

Wuthering Heights was the only novel of Emily Brontë (1818–48), one of three famous novelist sisters of the nineteenth century. She was two years younger than Charlotte, the writer of *Jane Eyre*, and a year and a half older than Anne, whose books are less well-known.

The three sisters grew up in the village of Haworth, Yorkshire, in northern England, where their father was a churchman. Their mother died in 1821, and they were educated at home. They read widely and created imaginary worlds about which they wrote stories and poems.

All three of the sisters began to write novels in 1844, and by the end of 1847 they had each sold their first book. While Charlotte's *Jane Eyre* was an immediate success, few readers understood *Wuthering Heights* at the time. Emily died a year later – never knowing how completely the public's attitudes were to change. After her death, respect for her work began to grow and she is now widely accepted as the greatest of all the Brontës. Her imaginative powers have even been compared to those of Shakespeare.

The following titles are available at Levels 4, 5 and 6:

Wuthering Heights

EMILY BRONTË

Level 6

Retold by John Escott
Series Editor: Derek Strange

PENGUIN BOOKS

Published by the Penguin Group
Penguin Books Ltd, 27 Wrights Lane, London W8 5TZ, England
Penguin Books USA Inc., 375 Hudson Street, New York, New York 10014, USA
Penguin Books Australia Ltd, Ringwood, Victoria, Australia
Penguin Books Canada Ltd, 10 Alcorn Avenue, Toronto, Ontario, Canada M4V 3B2
Penguin Books (NZ) Ltd, 182–190 Wairau Road, Auckland 10, New Zealand

Penguin Books Ltd, Registered Offices: Harmondsworth, Middlesex, England

Wuthering Heights was first published in 1847
This adaptation published by Penguin Books 1993
1 3 5 7 9 10 8 6 4 2

Text copyright © John Escott 1993
Illustrations copyright © Bob Harvey (Pennant Illustrators) 1993
All rights reserved

The moral right of the adapter and of the illustrator has been asserted

Illustrations by Bob Harvey

Typeset by Datix International Limited, Bungay, Suffolk
Printed in England by Clays Ltd, St Ives plc
Set in 11/14pt Lasercomp Bembo

To the teacher:

In addition to all the language forms of Levels One to Five, which are used again at this level of the series, the main verb forms and tenses used at Level Six are:

- future perfect verbs, passives with continuous or perfect aspects of the 'third' conditional with continuous forms
- modal verbs: *needn't* and *needn't have* (to express absence of necessity), *would* (to describe habitual past actions), *should* and *should have* (to express probability or failed expectation), *may have* and *might have* (to express possibility), *could have* and *would have* (to express past, unfulfilled possibility or likelihood).

Also used are:
- non-defining relative clauses.

Specific attention is paid to vocabulary development in the Vocabulary Work exercises at the end of the book. These exercises are aimed at training students to enlarge their vocabulary systematically through intelligent reading and effective use of a dictionary.

To the student:

Dictionary Words:
- As you read this book, you will find that some words are in darker black ink than the others on the page. Look them up in your dictionary, if you do not already know them, or try to guess the meaning of the words first, and then look them up later, to check.

The house stands high up on the wild moors
and is called Wuthering Heights.

MR LOCKWOOD'S STORY

1

1801 . . .

I have just returned from a visit to my landlord, Mr Heathcliff. Because of the heavy snow and strong winds, I was forced to stay the night.

And what a night!

The house stands high up on the wild **moors** and is called Wuthering Heights. A very suitable name since 'Wuthering' means 'blowing strongly'! But it is not the house, or even the dark, angry looks of Mr Heathcliff that will **haunt** me in the days to come. It is the dream I had while I slept in that room at the top of the house.

There were a few damp and dusty books on a **shelf** and I looked at some before settling down in my bed to sleep. The names Catherine Earnshaw or Catherine Heathcliff or Catherine Linton were written inside the books. And it was the name Catherine that remained with me as I fell asleep . . .

I could hear the sound of something knocking against the window. Thinking it was the branch of a tree outside, I reached out to open the window . . . and pushed my hand through the glass, breaking it. But it was not a tree branch that my fingers closed around, it was a tiny ice-cold hand! I tried to pull back my arm, but the hand would not let me go.

Now a voice was crying, 'Let me in! Let me in!'

'Who are you?' I asked.

'Catherine Linton,' it replied. 'I've come home. I lost my way on the moor. I've been lost for twenty long years.'

A child's face looked through the window, and I pulled its wrist on to the broken glass until blood was running down it. Still the hand would not let me go.

'Let me go if you want me to let you in!' I cried. And the

7

fingers relaxed. I quickly pulled my hand inside and pushed
some books against the hole in the window. 'Go away!' I
screamed. 'I'll never let you in!'

It was at that moment that I woke up – to find my landlord,
Mr Heathcliff, standing in the doorway of the room, holding a
candle. His face was white and filled with terror.

'It's only me, Lockwood, your guest,' I said. 'I've had a
terrible dream and must have cried out. This room is full of
ghosts. I'm not surprised that you usually keep it shut up.'

'What do you mean?' he wanted to know. 'What ghost?'

'The child said her name was Catherine Linton, and that
she'd been wandering around the moors for twenty years!'

It was then that I remembered the names written in the
books. One of them had been Catherine Linton. Was that how
I came to dream about the name?

'What can you mean?' shouted Heathcliff. 'You must be
mad!'

He seemed so upset that I said no more.

This morning, after breakfast, Mr Heathcliff accompanied
me across the moor, back to the garden of Thrushcross
Grange, a house which he owns and in which I am a **tenant** at
this time. We made very little conversation and said nothing
of my dream. But now I am curious about him and will ask my
housekeeper, Mrs Dean, to tell me about this strange man
and the house called Wuthering Heights.

1

Before I came to live at Thrushcross Grange, I was almost always at Wuthering Heights. Mr Earnshaw was the owner of the house, and my mother was one of his servants. He had a son, Hindley, and a daughter, Catherine. Whenever I was at the house, the three of us would play together.

One summer morning, when Catherine was only six, Mr Earnshaw went on a journey to Liverpool. He was gone for three days, but when he came back he was carrying something in his coat.

'Look!' he said to Mrs Earnshaw. And he opened his coat.

Inside, there was a dirty, black-haired child dressed in rags. It looked older than Catherine, but when Mr Earnshaw stood it on its feet it only stared at us and spoke words we could not understand.

I was frightened, and Mrs Earnshaw was ready to throw the child out of the house. But her husband explained how he had found it starving, without a home and half-dead in the streets of Liverpool. Nobody knew who the child belonged to, he said, so he brought it home with him.

'Wash him, Ellen,' the master told me. 'Give him clean things, and let him sleep with the children.'

But Hindley and Catherine refused to have the child in their room.

The boy was given the name of Heathcliff, which was the name of another son of Mr Earnshaw, a boy who had died. He was a **sullen**, patient child. Catherine became friendly with him, but Hindley always hated him. He often beat Heathcliff, but the boy took the blows without complaining and without crying, as if he was used to this sort of rough **treatment**.

Old Mr Earnshaw did not like the way his son treated Heathcliff; and Catherine was difficult with her sudden tempers and naughty ways. So Heathcliff soon became the old man's favourite child.

This made Hindley jealous and, when Mrs Earnshaw died two years later, Hindley hated Heathcliff more than ever. At the start I could understand and forgive Hindley's feelings, but then the children became ill and I began to see things differently.

I was given the job of looking after the children, and Hindley and Catherine were much trouble to me. But Heathcliff, who was dangerously ill, was as quiet and uncomplaining as a lamb.

'It was your care that saved his life, Ellen,' the doctor told me when Heathcliff was better.

But I could find nothing pleasant about the boy, and I could not understand Mr Earnshaw's love for him. Heathcliff never said a kind or grateful word to the old man.

2

As time passed, Mr Earnshaw's health began to fail. And when he could no longer go out, he became bad-tempered about the smallest thing. Hindley, especially, annoyed him and was eventually sent away to college.

But now it was Catherine who made certain that we had no peace in the house. A wild, wicked girl she was, but she had the sweetest smile and the prettiest eyes. I don't believe she really meant to do any harm.

Her poor father did not understand her. He especially did not understand her power over Heathcliff. She was rude to the boy, yet he always did what Catherine asked him to do. Mr Earnshaw was kind to him, but Heathcliff only obeyed the old man if he felt like doing so.

But the time came when Mr Earnshaw's troubles were ended. It was a wild and stormy October evening. A strong wind was blowing around the house and roaring in the chimney. He was sitting by the fire with Catherine at his feet. I remember he touched her hair and said, 'Why can't you always be a good girl, Cathy?'

She turned her face up to his and laughed. 'Why can't you always be a good man, father?' she answered. When she saw that he was angry, she kissed his hand and said she would sing him to sleep.

She began singing softly, till his fingers dropped from hers, and his head fell on to his breast. Joseph, Mr Earnshaw's old servant, stepped forward and called his master's name when it was time for bed and prayers. There was no reply, so Joseph moved the candle nearer and looked at the old man's face. I thought something was wrong when Joseph told the children that they must go upstairs and pray alone tonight.

'I shall say goodnight to father first,' said Catherine, putting her arms around his neck before anyone could stop her. And then she gave a scream. 'Oh, he's dead! Heathcliff, he's dead!'

Both children gave a heart-breaking cry.

◆

Hindley came home for the funeral – and surprised everyone by bringing a wife with him.

Everything in the house seemed to please her, except for the preparations for the funeral. These upset her badly and I asked her what was wrong.

'I'm so afraid of dying,' she told me.

It seemed silly to be thinking of such things when she was so young, but she was rather thin and did become breathless when she climbed stairs. She also had a cough which troubled her.

Hindley had changed considerably in three years. He spoke and dressed like the master of the house, which he was now. He ordered Joseph and me to stay in the back kitchen, and to leave the house to him. Heathcliff was ordered to do the same, so that the boy no longer felt part of the family but like a servant. His lessons with the **vicar** were stopped and he was put to work on the farm.

At first, Heathcliff did not mind. Cathy taught him what she learned, and worked or played with him in the fields. They often ran away to the moors and remained there all day, and then were punished for it when they got home. But this was forgotten the moment they were together again.

One Sunday evening, I went to call Catherine and Heathcliff for supper, but could not find them. We searched the house and **stables**, but they were nowhere to be seen.

'Lock the doors!' Hindley said, angrily. 'And nobody should let them in tonight.'

We went to our rooms, but I did not go to bed. Although it was raining outside, I opened my window. I wanted to hear if the young people came home.

But Heathcliff came alone. I ran downstairs and opened the door before the master heard him.

'Where is Miss Catherine?' I asked quickly.

'At Thrushcross Grange,' he answered. He took off his wet clothes and explained. 'We saw the lights, and Catherine and I went to see how the Lintons spent their Sunday evenings. We crept across the garden and looked in the lighted window. Edgar and his sister, Isabella, were alone. But were they happy? No. Isabella − she is eleven, a year younger than Cathy − was lying on the floor, screaming. Edgar was standing by the fire, crying silently. In the middle of the table was a little dog, and the two of them had been fighting over it! The **idiots**! Can you imagine me wanting something Catherine wished to have? Can you imagine us quarrelling? I wouldn't change places with Edgar Linton for anything – not even the chance to paint the house with Hindley's blood!'

'Don't say that!' I interrupted. 'Tell me why Catherine was left behind.'

'The Lintons heard us laughing and ran to the door. We heard a dog barking and began to run. I was holding Cathy's hand, but she fell down. "Run, Heathcliff, run!" she cried. I looked and saw that the dog had seized her ankle between its teeth. I swore at it, **thrust** a stone into its mouth, and tried to push it down its throat. A servant came with a lamp and pulled the dog away. Then he picked up Catherine and carried her into the house. I followed them, swearing.

'"What happened, Robert?" Mr Linton asked from the entrance. "The dog has caught a little girl, sir!" The servant said. "There's a boy with her. They must be thieves!" We were taken inside, and then Edgar recognized Catherine. "That's Miss Earnshaw," he whispered to his mother. "Miss Earnshaw?" cried Mrs Linton. "How can her brother allow her to run wild on the moors so soon after their father's death?" "And who's the boy?" said Mr Linton. "His language is terrible!" I began swearing again, and the servant was ordered to take me away. He pushed me out of the house and locked the door.'

'What about Catherine?' I said.

'I looked through the window and saw her sitting quietly on the sofa with Mrs Linton,' Heathcliff said. 'They were washing her foot and giving her something to eat. I could see that they admired her very much.'

'There will be trouble after this,' I told him.

I was right. Hindley was very angry. He told Heathcliff to keep away from Catherine, and not speak a word to her in the future.

3

Catherine stayed at Thrushcross Grange five weeks: till Christmas. By that time, her ankle was better and her manners were much improved. She wore pretty clothes and looked quite grown-up; no longer a wild little thing.

Hindley was delighted. 'Why Cathy, you are quite beautiful!' he said, lifting her from her horse when she arrived back at Wuthering Heights.

She kissed me, and then looked around for Heathcliff. At first, he was nowhere to be seen. While Catherine had been away, he had become dirtier and more wild-looking than ever, and he was ashamed to show himself to this bright and graceful young lady.

'Is Heathcliff not here?' she demanded, pulling off her gloves.

'Heathcliff, you may come forward,' said Hindley. 'You may welcome Miss Catherine home, like the other servants.'

Suddenly, Cathy saw her friend and ran towards him. She threw her arms around him and gave him seven or eight kisses, then stood back and looked at him. 'How very black and angry you look!' she said, laughing. 'And how funny! But that's because I'm used to Edgar and Isabella Linton. Well, Heathcliff, have you forgotten me?'

He tried to run away but Miss Cathy seized him.

'I did not mean to laugh at you,' she said. 'Why are you in a bad temper? It's only that you looked so odd. Wash your face and brush your hair, it will be all right.'

He pulled his hand away from her. 'I shall be as dirty as I like!' he shouted. And he ran from the room.

Hindley and his wife laughed at him, but Catherine could not understand what she had done to make Heathcliff so angry.

Later, I went outside to find Heathcliff. He was in the stables, feeding the horses.

'Hurry up, Heathcliff,' I said. 'You can come and sit by the fire and talk to Miss Cathy when she comes to the kitchen.'

He did not answer, and after five minutes I went back inside the house again. Heathcliff worked until nine o'clock, then he went to his bedroom.

◆

Edgar and Isabella Linton had been invited to Wuthering Heights on Christmas Day. In the morning, they went to church with the young Mr and Mrs Earnshaw and Catherine. Heathcliff stayed on the moors until they had all gone, then he came to see me.

'Ellen,' he said. 'Make me respectable, I'm going to be good.'

'It's time you were,' I told him. 'You've upset Catherine. Although I should be getting dinner ready, I'll take the time to make you clean and tidy.'

'I wish I was a gentleman, like Edgar Linton,' he said.

'You would be handsome if you stopped frowning,' I said, forcing him to look at himself in the mirror while I made him tidy. Slowly, he lost his frown and began to look quite pleasant.

We heard the sound of a carriage outside. Heathcliff ran to the window and I ran to the door, just in time to see Catherine leading the two Linton children towards the house.

'Hurry, Heathcliff!' I said. 'Go and greet them. Show them how nice you can look.'

But as he opened the kitchen door, he found Hindley on the other side. The master seemed annoyed to see him clean and smiling. He pushed Heathcliff back into the kitchen. 'Stay in here!' he said. Then he pulled Heathcliff's hair. 'You've combed it, have you? Then I'll pull it to make it a bit longer!'

'It's long enough already,' said a voice. It was Edgar Linton, and he was looking through the doorway. 'It's like horses' hair!'

Heathcliff seized a bowl of hot apple sauce from the kitchen table and threw it into Edgar's face. The boy began to cry loudly, which brought Catherine and Isabella to the scene. Hindley pushed Heathcliff up to his room, where he could punish him.

I washed Edgar's face while his sister began crying. Cathy watched us, ashamed of everybody.

'You should not have spoken to him,' she told Edgar. 'He was in a bad temper, and now you've spoilt your visit. He'll be beaten, and I hate him to be beaten!' She looked at Isabella. 'Be quiet! Nobody has hurt *you*!'

Hindley came back with a red face, and breathing hard. Then they all went in to their meal. I watched Catherine's unhappy face for the rest of that day. Then in the evening, she went up to Heathcliff's room and talked to him through the closed door. Later, I went up to warn her that the party was nearly over, and that the master would be looking for her. Instead of finding her outside Heathcliff's door, the little monkey was in his room! She had climbed in through a small window.

I persuaded her to come downstairs, but she brought Heathcliff with her. I took him to the kitchen and gave him some food, but his appetite was poor and he ate very little.

'What are you thinking about?' I asked him.

'I'm trying to decide how to punish Hindley,' he said. 'I don't care how long I have to wait, if I can only do it in the end. I hope he won't die before I do!'

4

On a fine June morning, Hindley's son, Hareton, was born. Young Mrs Earnshaw was very weak and ill afterwards, and

Heathcliff seized a bowl of hot apple sauce from the kitchen table and threw it into Edgar's face.

the doctor told Hindley that she would not live for very long.

Hindley swore about the doctor. 'Frances will be perfectly well in a week,' he told me.

But she was not. Nothing the doctor gave her could help. One night when she was coughing and Hindley was holding her in his arms, her face changed, and she was dead.

Hindley did not **weep** or pray; he swore and shouted at everyone. His moods became black and fierce, and all the servants left. Now there was only old Joseph and myself.

I was given the baby to look after. Hindley took no interest in his son. No respectable people came to the house any more, except for Edgar Linton, and he came to see Miss Cathy.

At fifteen she was the most beautiful girl in the neighbourhood – but she was proud and difficult, and I did not like her any more. She did not want Edgar and Heathcliff to meet when the young Linton came to visit, and kept them apart from each other. Heathcliff was sixteen, and did his best to be unpleasant to everyone. He stopped taking an interest in books or learning, and did not try to keep up with Catherine and her studying. They were still always together when he was not working, but he no longer expressed the way he felt about her.

Edgar Linton did not like coming to the house when Hindley was there. So one afternoon when Hindley was out, Catherine sent a message to Edgar telling him to come. She was waiting for him when Heathcliff came in.

'Cathy, are you busy this afternoon?' he asked.

'Isabella and Edgar Linton talked about coming,' she told him.

'Don't send me away because of those silly friends of yours!' he said. 'You spend so much time with them, and not me.'

'And why should I sit with you?' she demanded, angrily. 'What do you talk about? Nothing!'

At that moment, a horse was heard outside. Edgar Linton entered soon after, looking happy. Heathcliff's face was dark and sullen. No doubt Catherine noticed the difference between her two friends, as one came in and the other went out.

'Take yourself away, Ellen,' Miss Catherine told me. 'This is no time to be cleaning the room.'

'It's a good opportunity, now that the master is away,' I said. 'I'm sure Mr Edgar will not mind.'

Catherine came across and, making sure that Edgar could not see her, she pinched my arm.

'Oh, Miss!' I cried. 'That's a nasty trick! You've hurt my arm.'

'Don't lie, I didn't touch you!' she cried. But her face was red.

'What's that then?' I answered, showing them the red mark on my arm.

Before she could stop herself, she slapped me across the face.

'Catherine, love, Catherine!' said Edgar. He was shocked by her lying and her violence.

'Leave the room, Ellen!' she said, shaking with anger.

Little Hareton was with me, and began to cry. Miss Catherine seized his shoulders and began to shake him. Edgar laid a hand on her arm to stop her. In an instant, she turned and hit him hard on the ear.

Pale and angry, Edgar Linton picked up his hat.

'Where are you going?' Miss Catherine asked him. 'You must not go!'

'I must and shall,' he replied.

'No!' she cried. 'You can't leave me in that temper. I shall be miserable all night, and I won't be miserable for you!'

'I'm afraid and ashamed of you,' he said. 'I'll not come here again.'

'Go, if you like! And now I'll cry until I'm sick!' She dropped to her knees beside a chair, and began to weep loudly.

Edgar went out into the **courtyard** – but he came back again, unable to leave her like that. He went into the room and shut the door behind him.

Later, I went to tell them that Hindley had come home, and that he was drunk. I could see immediately that their quarrel had only brought them closer together. They were no longer friends, they were lovers.

◆

Hindley's drunken temper was fierce and terrible.

'It's a pity he can't kill himself with drink,' Heathcliff said later, when I was taking little Hareton to the kitchen. I thought Heathcliff went outside after this, but I was wrong. He sat down on the other side of the **settle** and remained silent, and I did not realize he was there.

Cathy waited until her drunken brother had gone to his room, then came to find me.

'Are you alone, Ellen?' she whispered.

'Yes, Miss,' I replied.

'Where's Heathcliff?'

'In the stables,' I answered, believing it to be true.

She came to kneel beside me. 'I'm very unhappy,' she said, looking so sad it was hard not to forgive the way she had treated me earlier. 'Will you keep a secret for me?'

'Is it worth keeping?' I said.

'Edgar Linton has asked me to marry him and I've agreed. Was I wrong?'

'Do you love him?' I asked.

'Of course I do,' she answered.

'Why do you?'

'Because he's handsome and he loves me,' she said. 'And because he will be rich and I shall be the greatest woman in the neighbourhood.'

'Then tell me why you are unhappy,' I said. 'Hindley will be pleased, and old Mr and Mrs Linton will not object to the marriage. Where is the problem?'

'Here!' she replied, putting her hand on her heart. 'In my heart and soul I'm sure I'm wrong to marry Edgar. If Hindley had not brought Heathcliff so low, I should not have thought of it. But how can I marry Heathcliff now? It would bring shame on me. So, he will never know how much I love him. Whatever our souls are made of, Ellen, his and mine are the same. He is more myself than I am.'

Before she stopped speaking, I realized Heathcliff was behind the settle. I saw him rise and walk out silently. He had listened until he heard Catherine say that marrying him would bring shame on her, then he could stay no longer.

Catherine did not hear or see him.

'As soon as you become Mrs Linton, Heathcliff will lose you,' I said. 'How will he bear the separation? How will you?'

'Who is to separate us?' she cried. 'I can help Heathcliff escape from my brother's power.'

'With your husband's money?' I said. 'He won't agree to that. And it's a very bad reason for being young Linton's wife.'

'I cannot stop loving Heathcliff. Ellen, I *am* Heathcliff! He is always, always in my mind.'

It was then that I told Catherine how I had seen Heathcliff leave the kitchen, and how he must have heard her talking about the shame marrying him would bring. Immediately, she jumped up and ran to look for him.

But although we searched the house and the stables, we

could not find him. Cathy would not come in, but waited for him by the wall near the road. Then about midnight, a storm came – thunder and a violent wind. Even then, Cathy would not come in until the storm was over. Her hair and clothes were very wet, but she would not get undressed or go to bed.

When I came down in the morning, she was still sitting in the kitchen.

Hindley was with her.

'What's the matter, Cathy?' he said. 'Why are you so pale and cold?'

She sat shaking, but would not tell him about Heathcliff.

'She's ill,' he said to me. 'I suppose that's the reason she would not go to bed. Or were you with Heathcliff last night?' he asked Catherine. 'Tell me the truth. I shall send him away this very morning.'

'I never saw Heathcliff last night,' answered Catherine. 'And if you send him away, I'll go with him. But perhaps he's already gone!' And she began to cry.

I helped her to her room where she became wild, and started screaming. I thought she was going mad, and I sent for the doctor. As soon as he saw her, he said she was dangerously ill and had a fever.

I cannot say I was a gentle nurse, but Joseph and the master were no better. Mrs Linton visited several times.

When Catherine was feeling a little better she was taken to Thrushcross Grange, and we were all very grateful. But poor Mrs Linton and her husband caught the fever, and they both died a few days later.

We heard nothing more of Heathcliff. He had disappeared.

Our young lady returned to us and was more difficult than ever. But the doctor said it was dangerous for her to be upset, so everyone did what she wished them to do.

5

Edgar Linton married Catherine Earnshaw three years later, in Gimmerton church. I was persuaded to go to Thrushcross Grange to live with them, and was surprised how quickly Catherine settled to her new life. She seemed very fond of Mr Linton, and fond of his sister, too.

They both did everything they could to make Catherine feel comfortable, and I noticed that Mr Edgar had a deep fear of making her angry. Catherine was sometimes silent and unhappy, but her husband thought this was due to the illness she had suffered. I believe they enjoyed a deep and growing happiness.

But it ended. On a warm evening in September, I was coming from the garden with a heavy basket of apples. I put it down on the step by the kitchen door and looked up at the moon. Suddenly, I heard a voice.

'Ellen, is that you?'

I turned and saw a man. Or was it a ghost? I thought. 'What?' I cried. 'You have come back? Is it really you?'

'Yes, it's me, Heathcliff,' he replied. 'Are they here? Where is she? I want to have one word with her. Tell her some person from Gimmerton wishes to see her.'

'How can I?' I said. 'She will be shocked. You *are* Heathcliff, but you're different. You've changed.'

'Take my message. I'm in hell until you do!'

We went inside and I went up to the living-room. Edgar and Catherine were sitting together peacefully, and I did not want to give them the message.

'A person from Gimmerton wishes to see you,' I told Catherine.

'What does he want?' asked Mrs Linton.

'I did not ask him,' I said.

She went downstairs and I closed the curtains.

'Who is it?' Mr Linton asked.

'Someone she does not expect,' I said. 'Heathcliff – you remember, sir? He used to live at Mr Earnshaw's house.'

'What, the servant, the farm boy?' he exclaimed.

'You must not call him by those names, master,' I said. 'It will upset her.'

At that moment, she ran into the room and threw her arms around her husband. 'Edgar, Edgar! Heathcliff's come back! I know you didn't like him, but you must be friends now, to please me. Shall I tell him to come up?'

'Up here?' said her husband. 'The kitchen is a more suitable place for him.'

'No, I can't sit in the kitchen,' she said. She laughed, and said to me, 'Ellen, set two tables. One for your master and Miss Isabella, the other for Heathcliff and myself.'

She was going to run off again, but Edgar stopped her. 'You tell him to come up, Ellen,' he said. 'And Catherine, try not to be silly. There is no need to welcome a runaway servant like a brother!'

Heathcliff was waiting downstairs and he followed me up to the living-room. He had grown into a tall, well-shaped man with the manners of a gentleman, but his eyes were still full of black fire. Next to him, my master looked much younger and smaller, and did not seem to know what to say.

'Sit down, sir,' he said, at last.

Heathcliff sat opposite Catherine, and she kept her eyes fixed on him as if afraid he might go away again. He gave her a quick glance now and then, and with each glance his face showed more and more delight. But not Mr Edgar. He became annoyed, and his face grew pale when he saw Catherine jump up and seize Heathcliff's hands again.

'I shall think this is a dream tomorrow,' she said, laughing wildly. 'I shall not be able to believe I've seen you and touched and spoken to you again. And yet, cruel Heathcliff, you do not deserve this welcome. To stay away for three years and never think of me!'

'A little more than you have thought of me,' he said. 'I heard of your marriage not long ago. I wanted to see your face once more, and to take my revenge on Hindley before killing myself. But your welcome has put these ideas out of my mind. You'll not drive me away again.'

Miss Isabella came to have tea, but the meal did not last more than ten minutes. Catherine was too excited to eat or drink.

'Are you going to Gimmerton?' I asked Heathcliff, when he left an hour later.

'No, to Wuthering Heights. Hindley Earnshaw invited me when I went there this morning.'

I could not understand this. Hindley Earnshaw invited *him*? He was going to Wuthering Heights, where he had been so unhappy? It was Catherine who explained it when she came to my room and woke me up in the middle of the night.

'I can't sleep, Ellen,' she said, 'and I want to talk to someone. Edgar is miserable because I'm glad Heathcliff has come back. He complains of a headache and will not talk. So I got up and left him.'

'What do you think about Heathcliff going to Wuthering Heights?' I asked.

'I wondered about that, too,' she said. 'He said he went there to find you, Ellen, and to ask you for information about me. Hindley was playing cards with some friends, and he asked Heathcliff to join them. My brother lost some money to Heathcliff, and then asked him to come back again in the evening so that he could win it back. Heathcliff agreed. He wants to stay at Wuthering Heights to be near me. He has money now and will offer Hindley a generous amount to stay there, and Hindley will be greedy enough to accept it.'

I was sure this would bring trouble, but I did not say so.

6

Heathcliff was cautious about coming to Thrushcross
e. He did not come too often, and Catherine realized it
wiser not to show too much pleasure when he did. And
slowly, my master came to accept the visits.

The trouble came when Isabella Linton fell in love with
Heathcliff.

At that time, she was a pretty young lady of eighteen. She
was pleasant and amusing, but had a short temper if people
annoyed her.

We had all noticed that there was something wrong. She
had grown pale and thin since Heathcliff had been coming to
the house.

'Go to bed,' Catherine told her one day, after Isabella had
been particularly bad-tempered and had complained of being
cold. 'I'll send for the doctor.'

'I don't need a doctor!' cried Isabella. 'It's you who makes
me ill and unhappy.'

'How can you say that?' said Catherine. 'When have I
made you unhappy?'

'Yesterday, when we walked across the moor,' said Isabella.
'You sent me off and walked with Mr Heathcliff, when you
knew I wanted to be with him. I love him! I love him more
than you ever loved Edgar. And he might love me, if you
would let him!'

'Ellen, tell her she is mad!' said Catherine. 'Tell her she is
an idiot not to see that Heathcliff is a fierce, cruel man
without pity. He would crush you like a bird's egg if he
became tired of you, Isabella. He couldn't love a Linton, but
he would be happy to marry you for your money.'

'How can you say such a thing! You are worse than his
worst enemy,' said Isabella. 'And you're lying!'

'Forget him, Miss,' I told her. 'Mrs Linton is speaking the

truth. Honest people don't have secrets. How has Heathcliff been living? How has he got rich? Why is he staying at the house of a man he hates? They say Mr Earnshaw sits up all night with him, playing cards, drinking and losing money. What sort of person takes money from a drunken man? Surely you don't want a husband like that?'

'I won't listen to your wicked talk!' cried Isabella.

But the next day, Catherine and Isabella were sitting together when Heathcliff arrived. Mr Linton was out.

'Come in, Heathcliff!' said Catherine, laughing. 'Here is someone who is breaking her heart over your beauty! No, no, don't run away, Isabella.' Catherine held the other woman's arm so that she could not move. 'We were quarrelling like cats about you, Heathcliff. She tells me that if I have the good manners to leave you alone, you will be unable to stop loving her. She was angry because I did not leave the two of you alone on the moor the other day.'

'I don't think she wishes to be alone with me now,' said Heathcliff. He stared at Isabella until the poor thing's face became white, then red, and tears came into her eyes. At last, she dug her fingernails into Catherine's hand so that the other woman was forced to release her.

'Why did you say that, Catherine?' Heathcliff asked, after Isabella ran out of the room. 'It wasn't true, was it?'

'It certainly was,' said Catherine.

There was a short silence, then Heathcliff said, 'She's her brother's **heir**, isn't she? Thrushcross Grange will be hers if he dies.'

'It will if I have no sons,' said Catherine. 'But I hope to have five or six. Forget it, Heathcliff. You are too quick to want your neighbour's goods; remember, *this* neighbour's goods are mine.'

'If they were mine, they would still be yours,' said Heathcliff. 'But you are right, we will forget it.'

27

They talked of it no more that day, but I was sure Heathcliff remembered it. His visits worried me, and I suspected that they worried my master, too.

◆

One day I went to Wuthering Heights. I wanted to see Hindley. We had been children together, had played together, and I could not help worrying about him. What if he were dead? Or dying?

There was a brown-eyed boy looking through the gate. It was Hareton.

'God **bless** you, Hareton,' I said. 'It's your nurse, Ellen.'

He moved away from the gate and picked up a large flat stone.

'I've come to see your father,' I said, realizing that he did not recognize me.

He threw the stone, and it knocked my hat off. Then he swore at me.

'Who taught you those fine words, my child?' I said, upset by his treatment of me.

'Devil Daddy,' was his answer.

'And who is that?'

'Heathcliff,' he said.

'Do you like Heathcliff?' I asked.

'Yes,' he said.

After this, I gave him an apple and told him to tell his father that a woman called Ellen Dean was at the gate. He took the apple and ran to the house. But instead of Hindley, it was Heathcliff who came to the door. Immediately, I turned and went quickly away.

The next time Heathcliff came to Thrushcross Grange, Miss Isabella was feeding some birds in the garden. He went straight across and spoke to her. I was standing by the kitchen window, but I moved away so that I could not be seen. He put a hand on her arm and glanced around to make sure nobody was watching them, then pulled her towards him and kissed her.

'You **scoundrel**!' I cried.

'Who is, Ellen?' said Catherine's voice at my elbow. I had been so busy watching Heathcliff and Isabella that I had not heard her come into the kitchen.

'Your friend,' I said. 'Oh, he's seen us and is coming in! What excuse will he have for kissing Isabella, when he told you he hated her?'

Isabella ran across the garden. A moment later, Heathcliff came in.

'I told you to leave Isabella alone,' Catherine said to him. 'If you don't, you will not be welcome here.'

'Why do you care?' he said angrily. 'I have a right to kiss her, if she chooses, and you have no right to object. I'm not *your* husband.'

'If you like Isabella, you shall marry her,' said Catherine. 'But do you like her? Tell the truth, Heathcliff! There, you won't answer.'

'If I thought you really wanted me to marry Isabella, I'd cut my throat!' said Heathcliff.

'You want to make trouble here,' she said. 'All right, quarrel with Edgar, and deceive his sister. That is the best way to take your revenge on me.'

The conversation stopped, and Catherine sat down by the fire, looking sad and angry. Heathcliff stood with folded arms, thinking his evil thoughts. And this was how I left them when I went upstairs to look for the master.

'Ellen, have you seen your mistress?' he asked, when I entered.

'She's in the kitchen, sir,' I said. 'She's upset by Mr Heathcliff's behaviour.' And I went on to explain what had happened in the garden. He was so angry, he had difficulty allowing me to finish.

'This is terrible!' he said. 'Call me two men from the servants' hall, Ellen.'

He descended to the kitchen and told the servants to wait outside. Catherine and Heathcliff were arguing again, but stopped when the master went in.

'You are poison in this house!' Edgar told Heathcliff. 'Get out now, you scoundrel!'

Heathcliff looked at Edgar and smiled. 'Cathy, this lamb of yours threatens like a lion. But he's not worth knocking down.'

My master signalled to me to fetch the men from outside, but Catherine shut the door and locked it before I had the chance.

'A fair fight!' she said, in answer to her husband's look of angry surprise.

Edgar tried to take the key from her, but she threw it into the fire. After this, Edgar began to shake, and his face became white with fear.

'You can have your coward, Cathy,' said Heathcliff. 'Is he weeping, or is he going to faint with fear?' He stepped forward and gave Edgar a push.

My master quickly gave Heathcliff a blow on the throat. It took Heathcliff's breath away, and Edgar used the time to walk out of the back door into the garden. From there he went on to the front entrance of the house.

'Go, Heathcliff!' cried Catherine. 'He'll come back with guns, and the servants!'

Heathcliff did not want to leave, but Catherine and I persuaded him to go. Then the two of us went upstairs, where Catherine threw herself on to the sofa.

'Tell Edgar I'm in danger of being seriously ill,' she ordered me. 'I want to frighten him, but I also hope it's true. What happened was not my fault. But if Heathcliff cannot be my friend, and if Edgar will be jealous and horrible, I'll break their hearts by breaking my own!'

My master quickly gave Heathcliff a blow on the throat.
It took Heathcliff's breath away.

I was leaving the room when Edgar came in.

'I'm not here to argue, Catherine,' he said. 'I just want an answer to a question. Will you now stop seeing Heathcliff, or will you stop seeing me? It is impossible for you to be *my* friend and *his* at the same time. I insist on knowing.'

'And I insist on being left alone!' cried Catherine. And she began to hit her head against the sofa.

Mr Linton suddenly looked afraid, and told me to fetch some water.

'There is nothing the matter with her,' I said, when I came back with the water. 'She wants to break your heart, and this is her way of doing it.'

Catherine immediately jumped up from the sofa, her eyes bright with anger. I expected her to hit me, but she ran up to her room and locked the door behind her. There she stayed for the next two days, refusing to eat or drink anything.

Mr Linton did not ask about her. He saw Isabella, but could get no sensible answers to his questions about her and Heathcliff. Finally, he warned her not to encourage that terrible man.

7

After that day, it seemed that I was the only sensible person at the Grange. Isabella walked around the park and garden, always silent and almost always weeping. Edgar sat alone with his books, and hoping – I guessed – that Catherine would come to him and ask to be forgiven.

Three days later, Catherine unlocked her door and asked me to bring her some water. Instead of just water, I brought her tea and bread, and she ate it hungrily.

'What is Edgar doing?' she asked me.

'He's reading his books in the library,' I informed her.

'Reading!' she cried. 'And I am dying! Does he not care?'

'He doesn't know you're sick, and he's not afraid that you'll die of hunger,' I said.

'Can't you tell him that I will?' she said.

'You have just eaten some food,' I reminded her. 'You'll feel better tomorrow.'

'If I could be sure it would kill him, I'd kill myself now!' she cried. 'I've not slept for three nights. I've been haunted, Ellen. But I can see you hate me like all the others.'

Madness came over her suddenly. She began to throw herself about on the bed; and she tore the pillow until the feathers burst out of it.

'Stop it!' I said.

She started to tremble, and took hold of my arm. Then, very slowly, the horror left her face and she began to look ashamed.

'Stay with me, Ellen,' she begged. 'I'm afraid to sleep, my dreams frighten me. Oh, if only I could be in my own bed in Wuthering Heights. I must see it! I must feel the wind on my face!'

Before I could stop her, she jumped out of her bed, ran to the window, and threw it open. The cold air swept into the room, as sharp as a knife. There was no moon, and everything beneath was in darkness. No light came from any house, far or near.

'Look!' she cried. 'That's my room with the candle in it, and the trees moving in front of it . . . and that other candle is in Joseph's room. How late he sits up! But Heathcliff, will you come? If you do, I'll keep you. They can bury me twelve feet under the ground, and throw the church on top of me, but I won't rest until you are with me.'

The door opened and Edgar came in.

'I heard voices . . . ' he began.

'Oh sir!' I cried. 'My poor mistress is ill. Forget your anger and persuade her to go back to bed.'

'Catherine ill?' he said, hurrying to her. Then he was silent; Mrs Linton's wild and haunted appearance shocked him. At last, he took her in his arms, and there was pain in his face as he looked at her.

'Oh, you've come, have you, Edgar Linton?' said Catherine, angrily. 'Why didn't you come before, when you were wanted? It's too late, now. Nothing can keep me from my grave in the **churchyard**. I'll be there before spring is over. Not with the Lintons under the church roof, but in the open air with a **headstone**. And you can please yourself whether you go to them or come to me when you die!'

'She has been talking nonsense all evening, sir,' I told Edgar. 'But let her rest and be looked after properly, and she'll be better.'

'I need no advice from you,' he answered. 'Why didn't you tell me how ill she was?'

'I didn't know that you wished to encourage her bad temper,' I exclaimed. 'Perhaps I should have pretended not to see Isabella and Mr Heathcliff, too. Next time, you can find these things out for yourself!'

'Oh, so it was *you* who told him, was it?' shouted Catherine. She tried to pull herself away from Edgar. 'Let me go, and she'll be sorry!'

I decided then to fetch the doctor, and hurried from the room.

I was on my way through the garden when I thought I heard the sound of a galloping horse. It was a strange sound to hear at two o'clock in the morning, but I was too busy worrying about Catherine to think about it.

The doctor walked back to Thrushcross Grange with me.

'I can't help thinking there must be another reason for Catherine's illness,' he said. 'How did it begin?'

'It began with a quarrel,' I told him. 'Then she refused to eat anything.'

'Has Heathcliff visited lately? I've heard that Isabella and Heathcliff were walking in the fields together for two hours last night. He wanted her to climb on his horse and ride away with him! The person who saw them said that she refused, but promised to be ready the next time he came.'

This filled me with fear as I remembered the horse I'd heard earlier. As soon as we were at the Grange, I went to Isabella's room – and found it empty.

It was the wrong time to tell Edgar, I decided; there was already enough for him to worry about. So I kept the news to myself.

The doctor told Edgar that Catherine must be kept calm and quiet. To me he said that madness was more of a danger for her than death.

It was the following morning when a servant told Edgar that Isabella had run away with Heathcliff. Someone had seen them riding through the village, soon after midnight.

'Well, it was her choice to go with him,' said Edgar. 'She had a right to go, if she pleased. Now don't speak to me about her again.'

8

For two months we heard no more about Heathcliff and Isabella. In that time, Catherine conquered the worst part of her illness. She was nursed day and night by Edgar, whose own health was sacrificed in the process, but who was full of joy when the doctor told him Catherine was out of danger.

Edgar brought her spring flowers and spoke with loving words, trying to make her cheerful. She was expecting a child, and this gave us all a reason to hope for her quick return to good health.

Isabella had sent a short letter to Edgar, telling him she was married. This happened six weeks after she left. Edgar did not reply to the letter, and just afterwards I received a letter from her myself. It said:

Dear Ellen

I came last night to Wuthering Heights and heard that Catherine has been very ill. I suppose I must not write to her, and my brother will not answer the letters I send to him, so I am writing to you. Tell Edgar that I would love to see him and Catherine again.

We are going to live here with Hindley and Hareton. A sullen ghost of a man, and a rude and bad-tempered boy! Please tell me, Ellen, how did you live here with these terrible people? And as for Heathcliff, I hate him! I have been a fool. Is he mad? Is he a devil? Please come to see me and explain. Don't write, but come with a letter from Edgar. Please!

Isabella

As soon as I finished reading this, I went to the master to tell him that his sister was now living at Wuthering Heights.

'She is sorry to hear Catherine has been ill,' I said. 'She wants to see you again. Can you write her a letter, forgiving her?'

'There is nothing to forgive,' he said. 'You may go to Wuthering Heights this afternoon and say that I am not *angry*, but that I'm *sorry* to have lost her. I will not go to see her. If she really wants to please me, then she should persuade that scoundrel she's married to leave the country.'

I went to Wuthering Heights that afternoon, without a letter. Edgar would not write one. Hindley was not at the house, but Heathcliff was. He was sitting with Isabella, and he offered me a chair in a friendly way.

'A stranger would think he was born a gentleman!' I thought when I saw him, for he looked proud of himself and was well-dressed. But Isabella looked pale and unhappy, and her clothes were old and dirty. She hurried forward, expecting me to give her a letter.

'If you have anything for Isabella, then give it to her,' said Heathcliff. 'We have no secrets between us.'

'Oh, I have nothing,' I replied. 'My master will not write or visit, but he sends his sister his love, and he wishes you happiness.'

Isabella looked ready to cry as she returned to her seat.

Heathcliff began to ask me questions about Catherine and her illness.

'She's better now, but she'll never be like she was,' I said. 'If you really care about her, you won't see her again, but will leave her to her husband.'

'Do you imagine I could leave Catherine to *him*?' replied Heathcliff. 'Before you leave this house, you will promise to ask her to see me.'

'She's nearly forgotten you,' I said. 'It will only make her ill again if you insist on seeing her.'

'You think that she has forgotten me? Oh, Ellen, you know that she has not! I would be in hell if I thought she had. And she loves Linton like she loves her dog or her horses. She can never love him the way she loves me.'

'Catherine and Edgar are as fond of each other as any two people can be!' cried Isabella.

'Your brother is not so fond of you,' said Heathcliff. 'Look how he turns you away!'

'He doesn't know what I suffer,' she said. 'I didn't tell him that.'

'You told him something then, did you?' said Heathcliff.

'I wrote to tell him we were married,' said Isabella. 'Nothing more.'

'My young lady looks unhappy,' I said. 'You must treat her kindly. She is used to having friends and a comfortable home.'

'She gave them up expecting me to be like the hero from a story-book,' he said. 'Now she knows me better. Today she told me that she hated me. But can I believe that? If she wants to leave here, she can.'

'He's lying, Ellen!' said Isabella. 'I've tried to leave him before — but I dare not try it again! But promise you'll say nothing to Edgar. Heathcliff says he's married me to get power over Edgar, but I won't let him. I'll die first!'

'Go upstairs,' Heathcliff told her, and thrust her from the room. 'I have something to say to Ellen.'

I was putting on my hat, getting ready to go.

'Put that down,' he told me. 'You're not going yet. You must help me see Catherine, without delay. I want her to tell me how she is, and why she's been ill. Last night I was in the Grange garden for six hours, and I'll return there tonight. I'll haunt the place, night and day, until I find an opportunity of entering. If Edgar sees me, I'll knock him down. But you can prevent that, Ellen. You can let me in when she is alone.'

'I won't do it,' I said. 'The shock would be too much for her.'

'You're not going back there until you agree,' Heathcliff told me, angrily. 'It's foolish to say that Catherine could not bear to see me. She'll not be completely well *until* she sees me, don't you understand? Now, will you help me, or must I keep you here?'

I refused him many times, but eventually he forced me to help him. I was to take a letter to Catherine, and then tell him when she was alone, if she agreed to see him.

9

I kept Heathcliff's letter for three days. I knew Heathcliff was somewhere in the garden for much of this time, but I wanted to wait until Edgar was out of the house. The fourth day was Sunday, and my master went to church with the servants. It was then that I took Heathcliff's letter to Catherine.

She was sitting beside her open bedroom window in a white dress. Her eyes were sad and they stared into the distance, as if she was in another world. A book lay in front of her, but she was not reading it.

'There's a letter for you, Mrs Linton,' I said gently. 'Shall I open it for you?'

'Yes,' she answered, without looking at me.

I opened it – it was very short. 'Now, read it,' I said. 'It's from Mr Heathcliff.'

She looked at the letter, and at the signature, then gave a sigh.

'He's in the garden,' I said, 'waiting for an answer.'

But Heathcliff was already in the hall, and moments later came into the room. He went straight to Catherine and took her in his arms.

One look told him she was going to die, and he could hardly bear to see her face. He held her close, kissing her again and again.

'Oh, Cathy! Oh, my life! How can I bear it?' he cried.

'What now?' said Catherine, suddenly angry. 'You and Edgar have broken my heart, Heathcliff! And you both come expecting to be pitied. I shan't pity you. How strong you are! How many years will you live after I've gone?'

Heathcliff was kneeling beside her; he attempted to rise, but she seized his hair and kept him down.

'I wish I could hold you until we were both dead,' she continued. 'I wouldn't care what you suffered. I suffer! Will you forget me? Will you be happy when I'm in the earth?'

Heathcliff pulled himself up and took her arm. 'How can you talk like that when you are dying?' he said, angrily. 'Your cruel words will haunt me for ever. I can never forget you, Catherine. While you are at peace in your grave, I shall suffer the pains of hell!'

'I'll not be at peace,' said Catherine. 'I'll suffer too, because we are parted. Please, forgive me!'

He stood behind her chair, hiding his face from her. She turned to look at him, but he walked to the **fireplace** and stood silently with his back to us. Catherine watched him for some minutes.

'You see, Ellen?' she said. 'He won't forgive me, not even to keep me out of my grave. *That* is how I'm loved! Well, never mind. That's not *my* Heathcliff. I shall love mine still, and take him with me. He's in my soul.' Her voice became puzzled. 'Why won't he be near me? I thought he wanted that. Heathcliff, dear! Don't be angry now. Do come to me, Heathcliff.'

She stood eagerly and supported herself on the arm of the chair. He turned and gave her a desperate look, his eyes wet at last. Catherine half-fell towards him, and he caught her. They were locked together so tightly that I thought my mistress would never be released alive.

Heathcliff sat down in the nearest seat, holding her against him. I moved towards him to see if she had fainted, but he waved me away. Then she lifted a hand and put it around his neck. She brought her cheek up to his and he covered her with kisses.

'Why did you despise me?' he asked, wildly. 'Why did you betray your own heart, Cathy? You have killed yourself. You loved me – then what *right* had you to leave me? I've not broken your heart, *you* have broken it, and you've broken mine. Do I want to live? What kind of living will it be when you – oh, God! Would *you* like to live with your soul in the grave?'

'Leave me alone,' cried Catherine. 'If I've done wrong, I'm dying for it. It's enough! You left me, too, but I forgive you. Now, forgive me!'

'It is hard to forgive, and to look at those eyes, and to feel those thin hands,' he answered. 'I forgive what you have done to me, but not what you have done to yourself.'

Heathcliff sat down in the nearest seat, holding her against him.

They were silent – their faces hidden against each other, and washed by each other's tears.

I grew anxious about the time. 'My master will be here soon,' I told them.

Heathcliff pulled Catherine closer to him and said nothing.

Then I saw a group of servants coming up the road. Mr Linton was not far behind. He opened the gate and walked towards the house.

'He's here!' I said urgently. 'Go quickly!'

'I must go, Cathy,' said Heathcliff. 'But, if I live, I'll see you again before you sleep. I'll stay near to your window.'

'You must not go!' she answered, and held him tight against her.

'I *must* – Linton will be here in a moment,' he said.

'No!' she cried. 'Don't go! I shall die! I shall die!'

Heathcliff sat back in his seat again. 'I'll stay, Catherine. I'll stay.'

I could hear my master coming up the stairs. Then I saw that Catherine's arms had fallen loose, and her head had dropped down. 'She's fainted . . . or dead,' I thought.

Edgar came into the room, and became crazy with anger when he saw Heathcliff. He took a step towards him, but Heathcliff stopped him by putting Catherine into Edgar's arms.

'Help her first, then speak to me,' said Heathcliff.

He walked into the sitting-room. Mr Linton called me, and we managed to help Catherine wake from her faint. Edgar was so worried about her that he forgot about Heathcliff. I did not. I went into the other room and told him Catherine was better.

'Go now,' I said. 'I'll tell you how she is tomorrow.'

'I'll go,' he said, 'but I shall stay in the garden. Be sure to keep your promise tomorrow, Ellen. If you don't, I shall come to the house again whether Linton is here or not.'

10

At twelve o'clock that night, Catherine gave birth to a daughter – a tiny child, born two months early. Two hours later, Catherine herself died. Edgar's sadness was made worse by her dying without leaving him a son and heir. Now, everything he owned would pass to his sister.

Next morning, I went to find Heathcliff in the garden where he was standing next to an old tree, some distance from the house.

'She's dead!' he said, when he saw me. 'I don't need you to tell me. Put your handkerchief away, she wants none of *your* tears.'

'Yes, she's dead,' I answered.

'How did –' He tried to say her name, but could not. 'How did she die?'

'Quietly as a lamb,' I answered.

'And – and did she ever say my name?'

'She knew nobody after you left her,' I said. 'She lies with a sweet smile on her face. Her life ended in a gentle dream, and I hope she may wake as gently in another world.'

'May she wake in hell!' he cried, violently. 'Oh, Catherine! Don't leave me where I cannot find you! I cannot live without my life! I cannot live without my soul!'

He hit his head against the tree, where there were marks of blood already. I guessed he had done this many times during the night.

'Go away!' he shouted at me. 'Leave me alone!'

There was nothing I could do for him, so I went.

◆

Mrs Linton was buried the Friday after her death. Mr Hindley Earnshaw was invited to his sister's funeral, but he did not come. Isabella was not invited.

Catherine's grave was dug on the green slope, in a corner of the churchyard. It was close to the moor which she loved so much.

Snow came to the moors the day after the funeral. I was watching it fall as I sat with the crying baby on my knee in the sitting-room. Suddenly, the door burst open and someone came in. It was Isabella.

She came across to the fire, and her breath came in short gasps when she spoke. 'I've run the whole way from Wuthering Heights,' she told me. 'Oh, I'm aching all over! And I've fallen many times on the way.'

Her hair and clothes were wet from the snow, and her face was scratched and bruised. I persuaded her to put on some dry clothes, then I washed the blood from her face.

'Now, what's happened?' I wanted to know.

'There's been a terrible quarrel,' she said. 'Hindley had a gun and was going to kill Heathcliff, but Heathcliff was too strong for him and took the gun away. I was frightened, Ellen. I can't stay at Wuthering Heights another night! But neither can I stay here – Heathcliff will come and find me. Please, get one of the servants to take me to Gimmerton.'

She would stay only as long as it took me to pack a few clothes for her, then she was gone. Nor did she stay at Gimmerton, but went farther south to make a new home near London. She was never to return to Wuthering Heights. Later, I heard she gave birth to a son, a few months after her escape. She gave him the name Linton.

I met Heathcliff in the village one day, and he asked me where Isabella was living. I refused to tall him.

'It doesn't matter,' he said, carelessly.

But a servant told him her address, and that she had had a child. After that, he would often ask me about the child when he saw me. When he heard the boy's name, he smiled.

'She wants me to hate it too, does she?' he said.

'I don't think she wants you to know anything about it,' I said.

'But I'll have it,' he said, 'when I want it. They can be sure of that.'

On the day after Isabella's unexpected visit, I told Edgar that she had left Wuthering Heights. I could see he was pleased that his sister had left Heathcliff, whom he hated and avoided. In fact, Edgar stopped going to many places after Catherine died. He stopped going to the village or the church, and instead he passed the time walking on the moors or going to his wife's grave. His greatest comfort now was his daughter. She was named Catherine, but he called her Cathy.

Six months after Catherine died, the doctor came to tell me Hindley Earnshaw was dead, too.

'It was drink that killed him,' said the doctor. 'He was only twenty-seven, the same age as you, Ellen.'

It was a great shock to me. But a greater shock came when I learned that Wuthering Heights would not belong to Hindley's son, Hareton. It was now Heathcliff's. Hindley had lost everything to him playing cards.

I went to see Heathcliff.

'Hareton must come and live at Thrushcross Grange, sir,' I said.

'Does Linton say that?' he demanded.

'Yes,' I said.

'If you take Hareton,' said Heathcliff, 'I shall replace him with my own son! Tell your master that!'

It was enough to stop Edgar. Heathcliff was now master of Wuthering Heights, and Hareton became like a servant to him.

11

The next twelve years at Thrushcross Grange were the

happiest of my life. Little Cathy brought joy into that sad house. She grew into a beautiful child, with a loving heart and a gentle voice. But if a servant upset her, or she did not get something that she wanted, she would say, 'I shall tell papa!'

I don't think her father ever spoke an angry word to her. Edgar taught her all her lessons, and enjoyed every moment he was with her. Till she reached the age of thirteen, she did not go beyond the park alone. Edgar took her a mile or two outside occasionally, but he trusted nobody else to go with her. She knew nothing of Wuthering Heights or Mr Heathcliff.

Most of the time Cathy was happy with things the way they were, but sometimes she would look out of the window and say, 'I wonder what is on the other side of those hills. Is it the sea, Ellen?'

'No, Miss Cathy,' I would answer. 'It's more hills.'

'And why are those rocks still bright so long after it is evening here?' The rocks were on the line of hills called Penistone Craggs.

'Because they are higher up than we are,' I explained. 'You could not climb them, they are too high and steep. In winter, the frost is there before it comes to us; and even in the summer I have found snow on the north-east side.'

'Oh, you have been on them! Then I can go, too, when I'm a woman. Has papa been there, Ellen?'

'Papa will tell you that they are not worth visiting,' I said quickly. 'The moors are much nicer, and Thrushcross park is the nicest place in the world.'

'But I know the park, and I don't know those,' she said to herself. 'My little horse, Minny, can take me.'

But her father would not let her go. 'You must wait until you are older,' he said.

The road to Penistone Craggs went close to Wuthering Heights, and Edgar could not bear to pass it. Whenever

Cathy asked if she was old enough to go, he answered, 'Not yet, love. Not yet.'

♦

Isabella lived for twelve years after she left Heathcliff and Wuthering Heights. She wrote to Edgar when she knew she was going to die, and asked him to come to her. She wanted to say goodbye to her brother, and to deliver her son, Linton, safely into his hands. She hoped that Linton could be left with him, and not with Heathcliff.

Edgar went without hesitation, and left Cathy with me. He gave orders that she was not to go out of the park, even with me, and never believed that she would go alone.

He was away three weeks. The first day or two, Cathy sat in a corner of the library, too sad to read or play. But then she became bored, and I sent her to walk or ride in the park. She pretended to be a traveller, and to have adventures. The days were warm and sunny, and sometimes she stayed out from breakfast until tea.

One morning Cathy said she was an explorer, and was going to cross the desert. 'I shall need plenty of food for myself and my animals,' she said. I gave her a basket of food, and she went off happily with her horse and three dogs. But she did not return for tea. The oldest dog returned, but not Cathy, her horse or the other two dogs.

I went to look for her. There was a man working on the fence around the park, and I asked him if he had seen her.

'I saw her this morning,' he replied. 'She jumped over the fence on her horse and rode away.'

I knew at once she would go to Penistone Craggs, and hurried off in that direction. The Craggs were half a mile from Wuthering Heights, and as I got near I saw one of the dogs. It was lying outside the house with blood on its ear.

I knocked on the door and it was opened by the house-keeper, a woman I knew.

'Ah, you've come for your little mistress!' she said. 'She's here safe. The master and Joseph are out. Come in and rest for a minute.'

I entered, and saw Cathy sitting in a little chair that had once been her mother's. Her hat was hanging on the wall, and she seemed perfectly at home. She was laughing and talking to Hareton – now a big, strong young man of eighteen. He stared at her curiously, and understood very few of the remarks and questions that were pouring from her.

I was relieved to find Cathy safe, but I hid my joy behind an angry face. 'Well, Miss!' I said. 'This is your last ride until papa comes back. I'll not trust you again, you naughty girl! Put on your hat and come home!'

She began to cry. 'What have I done? Papa won't be angry – he's never angry, like you!'

I picked up her hat and moved towards her, but she ran away and I was forced to chase her round the furniture. Hareton and the housekeeper began to laugh, and soon Cathy was laughing, too.

'Well, Miss Cathy, if you knew whose house this is, you'd be glad to get out,' I said.

'It's *your* father's, isn't it?' she said to Hareton.

'No,' he replied. His face became red and he looked at the floor.

'Whose, then – your master's?' she asked.

He swore and looked away.

'I thought he was the owner's son,' Cathy said to me. 'He talked about "our house", and he never called me "Miss", the way a servant does.'

Hareton grew as black as a thundercloud at this childish speech. I shook her silently, and got her ready to leave.

'Now, get my horse,' she said to Hareton, as if he was a servant at
the Grange. 'Hurry! What's the matter with you?'

'Now, get my horse,' she said to Hareton, as if he was a servant at the Grange. 'Hurry! What's the matter with you?'

'I'll see you in hell before I'll be *your* servant,' he shouted.

Cathy looked astonished. 'How dare he speak to me like that, Ellen?' She turned to the housekeeper. '*You* fetch my horse,' she said.

'You'll lose nothing by being polite, Miss,' said the woman. 'Mr Hareton is not the master's son, he's your cousin.'

'My cousin!' said Cathy. 'Oh, Ellen, don't let them say such things. Papa has gone to fetch my cousin from London. He's a gentleman's son.'

'People can have cousins of all sorts, Miss Cathy,' I said, 'without being any the worse for it.'

'He – he's not my cousin!' she cried, throwing herself into my arms and weeping.

Hareton's anger melted away when he saw her tears, and he went to fetch her horse. He was a good-looking young man, but was dressed in clothes suitable for working on the farm and not those of a gentleman. Nobody had taught him to read or write or how to behave.

On our way home, Cathy told me very little about her time at Wuthering Heights – only that her dogs had got into a fight with the farm dogs, and that was how she had met Hareton, and was then taken into the house.

I explained how her father objected to the people at Wuthering Heights. 'He'll be very sorry to hear you've been there,' I said, 'and he may blame me, and make me leave the Grange.'

'Then we won't tell him,' said Cathy. 'I couldn't bear it if you had to leave us, Ellen!'

12

A letter arrived from Edgar. Isabella was dead, and he was

bringing Linton back with him. Cathy went wild with joy when she heard her father was coming home.

'Linton is just six months younger than I am,' she said, excited about meeting her 'real' cousin.

Edgar greeted Cathy with as much excitement when they arrived. Linton was asleep in the corner of the carriage, and I looked in to see him. He was a pale, thin child, and was very much like Edgar, except that his face had a bad-tempered look that Edgar Linton's never had.

The child woke up and Edgar lifted him to the ground.

'This is your cousin Cathy,' he told the boy. 'She's fond of you already, so don't upset her by crying tonight. Try to be cheerful now. The travelling is over, and you've got nothing to do but rest and amuse yourself.'

They went into the library, where tea was laid out ready.

'He'll be all right, Ellen, if we can keep him,' Edgar said to me. 'He'll benefit from playing with a child his own age.'

'Yes, *if we can keep him*,' I thought to myself. 'But there's not much hope of that.'

And I was right.

Soon after the boy had gone to bed, Heathcliff's old servant, Joseph, arrived. He had come for Linton. Edgar refused to get the boy out of bed, but agreed to send him to Wuthering Heights the next day.

'Tell Mr Heathcliff that Linton's mother wanted him to stay with me,' Edgar said to Joseph. 'Tell him the boy is not well.'

But Heathcliff was determined to have the boy, and there was nothing Edgar could do. Next morning, very early and before Cathy was awake, I took Linton to Wuthering Heights. The boy was alarmed and confused.

'You're going to spend some time with your father, Mr Heathcliff,' I told him. 'He wants to see you very much.'

'My father!' he cried. 'Mother never told me I had a father.

Where does he live? Why haven't I heard of him before? I don't know him!'

I calmed him by saying that he would not have to stay at Wuthering Heights for long, and that Cathy and Mr Edgar would visit him.

'What is my father like?' he said.

I described Heathcliff's black hair and eyes.

'Then I'm not like him,' he said. 'How strange that he should never come to see mother.'

After that he rode Minny in silence, and I walked beside him.

Heathcliff had just finished breakfast when I opened the door. Joseph stood by his master's chair, and Hareton was getting ready to go out into the fields.

'Hallo, Ellen!' said Mr Heathcliff, when he saw me. 'You've brought him, have you? Let me see him.' He stared at Linton in silence, then laughed loudly. 'God, what a beauty! What a lovely thing! He's worse than I expected, Ellen, and I didn't expect much! Come here, boy!'

Linton hid his face in my shoulder and wept, but Heathcliff pulled the boy to him.

'None of that nonsense,' he said. 'We're not going to hurt you, Linton.' He took off the boy's hat and pushed back the fair hair. 'Do you know me?'

'No,' said Linton. He had stopped crying but he was still afraid.

'Well, I'm your father,' said Heathcliff. 'And your mother was a wicked woman not to tell you about me. Now, don't get angry, although it's good to see you have some temper. Be a good boy, and you'll be all right. Ellen, if you're tired you may sit down. If not, get home again.'

'I hope you'll be kind to the boy, Mr Heathcliff,' I said, 'or you won't keep him long. He's not strong.'

'I'll be *very* kind to him,' he said, laughing. 'Joseph, bring the boy some breakfast. Hareton, go to your work in the fields.' When they had gone, he turned to me again. 'Yes, Ellen, my son will be the owner of Thrushcross Grange, and I don't want him to die until I'm certain that it will pass from him to me. Besides, he's *mine*, and I want the pleasure of seeing *my* child lord of Edgar's land. He will have a room upstairs, and a teacher will come three times a week to give him his lessons. But he doesn't deserve all the trouble, he's such a miserable, pale-faced thing!'

Joseph returned with some breakfast and placed it in front of Linton. As the boy looked at it, I went quietly out of the door. But he heard me and cried out, 'Don't leave me! I won't stay here!'

But I climbed on to Minny and rode away without looking back.

◆

Cathy got up that day, eager to see her cousin. She was very upset when Edgar told her that the boy had gone away to live with his father. He did not say who the boy's father was, or where he was living.

Cathy wept and wept, until Edgar calmed her by saying, 'He'll come back soon.' But he was forced to add, 'If I can get him.' And there were no hopes of that.

Sometimes, I saw the housekeeper of Wuthering Heights in Gimmerton. She gave me news of Linton, and I learned that his health was still not strong. She also told me that Heathcliff disliked the boy even more, and could not bear to be in the same room with him.

'He's a selfish little boy,' said the housekeeper. 'He sits wrapped up in a coat beside the fire. And if Hareton tries to amuse him, the boy cries.'

Two years later, the housekeeper left Wuthering Heights and I was unable to get any more information about Linton.

13

Cathy slowly forgot about Linton, and time passed pleasantly at the Grange – until one fine spring morning when Cathy was sixteen.

'Hurry, Ellen!' she said. 'Father has said we can go for a walk on the moors, and there are some birds I want to see.'

I put on my hat and followed her out into the warm sun. She was a happy child in those days. She laughed and danced across the moor, her hair flying loose behind her. But there were many hills and banks to climb, and I began to get tired.

'Wait for me!' I called to her, but she did not seem to hear.

When I next saw her, she was on Wuthering Heights land, and she was talking with two people. As I got closer, I saw that it was Heathcliff and Hareton.

'Who are you?' Cathy was asking Heathcliff. Then she pointed at Hareton. 'I've seen him before. Is he your son?'

'Miss Cathy!' I said urgently. 'We must go back!'

'No, he's not my son,' answered Heathcliff. 'But I have one, and you've seen him before, too. Why don't you come to my house for a little rest?'

'No!' I said.

'Why not, Ellen?' said Cathy. 'I'm tired of running. And he says I've seen his son, although I think he's wrong. But I can guess where he lives. It's at the farmhouse that I visited when I went to Penistone Craggs, isn't it?'

I tried to stop her, but she was already walking towards the farmhouse.

'Mr Heathcliff, this is very wrong,' I said. 'She'll see Linton, and find out –'

'I want her to see Linton,' he answered. 'And we'll soon persuade her to keep the visit a secret.'

'I'm sure you have a bad plan,' I said.

'My plan is perfectly honest,' he replied. 'I hope the two

cousins will fall in love and get married. This is a generous act of mine. If the girl's father dies now, she will get nothing. If she marries Linton, she will join him as heir to her father's property.'

'And if Linton died,' I said, 'Cathy would be the heir.'

'No, she would not,' he said. 'His property would go to me. But to stop any arguments, I'm determined that the two shall marry.'

'And I'm determined that she'll never come here again,' I said.

We followed Cathy to the house. Heathcliff smiled and softened his voice when he spoke to her; and I was foolish enough to imagine that the memory of her mother would stop him harming her.

Linton was inside, sitting next to the fire. He was not quite sixteen, but tall for his age.

'Now, who is that?' Heathcliff asked Cathy. 'Linton, don't you remember your cousin?'

'Linton?' said Cathy, joyfully. 'Is that little Linton? He's taller than I am!'

She kissed him warmly and they stood looking at each other, for time had changed them both. Heathcliff watched them. Then Cathy went across to him.

'Are you my uncle, then?' she cried, reaching up to kiss him. 'Why don't you visit us at the Grange with Linton?'

'I visited it once or twice, before you were born,' said Heathcliff. 'But Mr Linton doesn't like me. We had a quarrel. So you must not tell him you have been here or he'll stop you coming again.'

'Why did you quarrel?'

'He thought I was too poor to marry his sister, and he was upset when I did,' said Heathcliff.

'That was wrong!' said Cathy. 'But Linton and I are not part of your quarrel. I won't come here, then. He can come to the Grange.'

'To walk four miles would kill me,' said Linton. 'No, come here, Miss Catherine. Not every morning, but once or twice a week.'

Heathcliff listened to his son and looked disgusted. 'Have you nothing to show your cousin on the farm?' he said, **scornfully**. 'Take her into the garden, and to see your horse.'

'Wouldn't you rather sit here?' said Linton, looking at Cathy.

'I don't know,' she said. But she looked at the door, eager to be active.

Linton moved closer to the fire. Heathcliff went to the door and called Hareton, and the other young man came in. He had washed himself, and his hair was still wet.

'Oh, I'll ask *you*, uncle,' said Cathy, remembering the housekeeper's words. 'He is not my cousin, is he?'

'Yes, he's your mother's nephew,' replied Heathcliff. 'Don't you like him? Hareton, take your cousin round the farm. And behave like a gentleman! Don't use bad language or stare at the young lady. Speak slowly and keep your hands out of your pockets. Entertain her as nicely as you can.'

He watched them go past the window. Then he turned to Linton, who was now looking sorry that he had missed the chance of walking with Cathy.

'Get up, you idle boy!' said Heathcliff. 'Go after them!'

Linton moved away from the fire and went outside. As he opened the door, I heard Cathy asking Hareton a question.

'What are those words cut in the stone over the door?' she said.

'I – I can't read it,' he said after a moment.

'Can't read it?' cried Cathy. 'I can read it. But I want to know why it's there.'

Linton laughed. 'Hareton can't read,' he said.

'Is he an idiot?' said Cathy. 'Or is there something wrong with his mind? I don't think he understands me when I ask him a question.'

Linton laughed again. 'You're just lazy, aren't you, Hareton? But your cousin thinks you're a fool.'

Hareton looked embarrassed and angry. 'If you weren't more like a girl than a boy, I'd knock you down!' he shouted. Then he left them.

We stayed until the afternoon, then walked home. Cathy did not see her father that night, so it was the next day when she told him about our visit to Wuthering Heights.

'Mr Heathcliff says you don't like him because he married your sister,' said Cathy. 'It's your fault that we're not all friends.'

Then Edgar told her how Heathcliff had treated Isabella, and how and why the man took Wuthering Heights from Hindley. Cathy was shocked and silent for some hours after that.

That evening, I found her crying in her bedroom.

'Linton expects me to come to him tomorrow,' she said. 'He'll wait for me, and when I don't come he'll be disappointed and unhappy.'

'Nonsense!' I said. 'He won't even think about it.'

'Can't I write him a letter to tell him why I can't come?'

'No, indeed!' I said. 'He would then write to you, and there would be no end to it.'

But she did write to Linton. She secretly sent him a letter, using a servant to deliver it. Linton answered her letter, and for six weeks letters were passed between them every day. When at last I discovered what was happening, I threatened to tell her father. Cathy wept, and said that she loved Linton. But no more letters were sent to Wuthering Heights.

14

Summer ended and autumn came. Cathy and her father often went for long walks. Her father noticed that she was quiet and sad, and he decided she must take more exercise in the fresh air. But one damp and cold day, they did not get back until the evening. My master caught a bad cold and became ill. After that, the doctor would not allow him to go out.

On an afternoon in October, Cathy and I went for a walk across the moors, and we met Heathcliff. He was riding his horse.

'I'm pleased to see you,' he said to Cathy.

'I shan't speak to you, Mr Heathcliff,' answered Cathy. 'Papa says you're a wicked man.'

'But I want to speak to you about Linton,' said Heathcliff. 'He was very upset when you stopped writing to him. He was in love, and you have broken his heart. As true as I live, he's dying for love of you! He'll be in his grave before next summer, unless you do something.'

'Don't lie to the poor child!' I said.

'It's no lie,' he said to me. 'I'm away until this time next week. You can walk over and see him yourselves. Surely your master would not object to her visiting her cousin!'

He rode off and we went back to Thrushcross Grange. As we walked, I looked at Cathy's sad face. She was thinking about Linton, and I knew before she spoke what she was going to say.

'I shan't be happy until I see him myself,' she said. 'I must tell Linton it's not my fault that I don't write.'

I could not bear to see her so sad, so I agreed to go with her to Wuthering Heights the next day.

Linton was sitting in a chair when we went in. As soon as Cathy saw him, she ran towards him.

'Is that you, Miss Linton?' he said, lifting his head from the chair. 'No – don't kiss me, it takes my breath. Papa said you would come. Please, shut the door. It's so cold!'

'Are you glad to see me, Linton?' said Cathy.

'Why didn't you come before?' he said. 'It made me very

tired writing those long letters. You should have come. Papa said it was my own fault. He called me a pitiful, worthless thing and said you despised me. You don't despise me, do you, Miss –?'

'I wish you would call me Cathy,' she said. 'Despise you? No! Next to papa and Ellen, I love you better than anybody alive.' She stroked his long, soft hair. 'Pretty Linton! I wish you were my brother.'

'I wish you were my wife,' said Linton.

Cathy looked serious. 'People hate their wives, sometimes, but not their brothers and sisters.'

'People don't hate their wives,' said Linton.

'Oh, they do! Your father hated your mother. Papa told me.'

'Well, I'll tell *you* something,' he said. 'Your mother hated your father!'

'Oh!' cried Cathy.

'And she loved mine!' he added.

'That's a lie!' shouted Cathy. And she pushed his chair so violently that he fell against one arm of it and immediately began coughing. He coughed for so long that it frightened me and made Cathy cry.

'I'm sorry I hurt you, Linton,' she said, when he stopped coughing.

'I can't speak to you,' he said. 'Now I shall lie awake all night coughing. Let me alone. I can't bear your talking.'

Cathy did not want to go, but he did not look up or speak again. We went to the door, but were stopped by a scream. Linton was lying on the fireplace, crying like a silly child. Cathy ran back and tried to calm him.

'I'll lift him on to the settle,' I said. 'Come away and leave him. He'll stop crying when there's nobody to listen to him.'

But Cathy stayed until we heard Hareton returning for his dinner.

'Will you come tomorrow, Cathy?' asked Linton.

'No,' I answered for her. 'Not tomorrow or the next day.'
But Cathy whispered something in his ear, and he smiled.
We left Wuthering Heights and walked home.

♦

The next day I was ill, and did not leave my room for three weeks. Cathy behaved like an angel. As soon as she left her father's room, she came to see me. Her days were divided between us, and she was a good nurse. But the evenings were her own, and I did not know how she spent them.

My answer came when I was able to get out of bed. Cathy was reading to me when she suddenly complained about having a headache. I told her to go and rest in her room, and later I went up to see if she was all right.

Her room was empty.

I waited. She returned much later, and she had been riding.

'Where have you been?' I asked her. 'And don't tell me any lies.'

'Promise not to be angry!' she begged. 'I've been to Wuthering Heights. I've been going since the day you became ill.'

She told me about her visits to Linton. Some of them were happy, others were spoilt by Linton behaving like a child or acting in a selfish manner. Sometimes they played games, or she sang pretty songs to him.

'One evening,' she told me, 'I met Hareton outside the house. He pointed up to the words in the stone over the door. "Miss Catherine! I can read that now!" he said. And then he read out the name, Hareton Earnshaw. I asked him to read the date, after his name. "I can't, yet," he said. And I laughed. Oh, what an idiot he is, Ellen!'

'No, Miss Cathy, dear,' I said. 'He was as quick and clever as you were when he was a child. And now he's trying to learn again. Don't despise him for that.'

'I haven't finished,' said Cathy. 'Soon after I laughed at

him, he came into the house and had a terrible quarrel with Linton. Linton became so angry that he started coughing. It was horrible! He fell on the ground and blood was coming from his mouth as he coughed. Joseph and the housekeeper took him to his room and I didn't see him again that night. But as I was leaving, I saw Hareton waiting for me outside. "Miss Linton, I'm sorry," he began. I didn't wait to listen. I hit him with my whip and rode away. Now you know everything, Ellen, but please don't tell papa!'

But I could not keep her secret. I told Edgar about her visits, and he stopped Cathy going to see Linton. She begged him to let her go to Wuthering Heights, but he refused. He wrote to Linton and told him that he could visit Cathy at Thrushcross Grange. He explained that Linton must not expect to see Cathy at Wuthering Heights again.

15

Linton did not come to the Grange. He wrote to say that Heathcliff objected to his coming. He asked if he could meet Cathy on the moors, but Edgar would not agree to this because he could not go with her.

Winter and spring passed, and Edgar became weaker. But it was summer before he finally said that I could go with Cathy, and that she could meet Linton on the moors.

But when we reached Linton, it was close to Wuthering Heights and he looked pale and ill.

Cathy gave a cry of alarm and asked him if he was worse than usual.

'No – better – better!' he gasped.

Cathy sat down beside him. She was disappointed to see him so ill, and in no mood to talk or listen. 'Perhaps Ellen and I should go home again,' she said.

'No, please!' he begged. 'Stay another half-hour!'

But before ten minutes passed, he was asleep.

We stayed with him until he was awake again, then Cathy said we must go.

'Wait!' he cried, and he grasped her arm. 'Listen! He's coming. Heathcliff's coming!'

Cathy pulled away from him when she heard this. 'I'll be here next Thursday,' she said. 'Goodbye. Hurry, Ellen!'

We left him waiting for his father.

♦

Seven days passed and Edgar became even weaker. Cathy knew he was dying and stayed with him almost all the time. When the next Thursday came, I reminded her of her appointment with Linton. She did not want to leave her father, but he thought she ought to go.

It was a golden August afternoon and the moors were beautiful, but Cathy scarcely looked at them. She was already regretting leaving her father.

Linton was waiting in the same place, but he did not look especially pleased to see us. In fact, he looked afraid.

'It's late!' he said. 'I thought you weren't coming.'

'Why don't you tell the truth?' said Cathy, angrily. 'Tell me you don't want me here! My father is ill and I've wasted my time coming!'

'Please, Cathy!' he cried. 'Don't be angry!' He threw himself on to the ground. 'I shall be killed if you leave me! My life is in your hands. And perhaps you will agree – and he'll let me die with you.'

'Agree to what?' asked Cathy, her anger melting away. 'To stay? Tell me the meaning of this strange talk, and I will.'

'I dare not tell,' said Linton. 'My father has threatened me!'

Cathy's anger returned. 'Oh, keep your secret!' she said.

He began to weep wildly and to kiss her hands. I was

wondering what the mystery was about when I heard a sound. I turned and saw Mr Heathcliff coming towards us.

'Well, Ellen,' he said, ignoring the other two. 'There are some rumours that Edgar Linton is on his death-bed. Is that true?'

'It's true,' I replied.

'How long will he last, do you think?' He looked at Linton. 'That boy seems determined to die first. I'll thank his uncle to be quick! Get up, Linton!'

Linton tried to stand but fell over on his back. Heathcliff went over and helped him to sit up.

'Take my hand and stand on your feet,' said Heathcliff, trying to control his anger. 'Now, Miss Catherine will give you her arm. Perhaps she will walk home with you.'

'I can't go to Wuthering Heights, Linton,' whispered Cathy. 'Papa has forbidden me. Why are you so afraid?'

Linton grasped her arm tightly and begged her to go with him. 'I – I can't go back without you!' he cried, wild with fear.

So Cathy and I went with him. We reached the doorway of the farmhouse and Cathy took Linton in to sit on a chair. I waited at the door for her to come out again, but Heathcliff pushed me forward.

'Go in, Ellen!' he said. 'Sit down and let me shut the door.'

He shut and locked the door, and I jumped with alarm.

'I'm by myself today,' he said. 'Hareton, Joseph and my housekeeper are out. Miss Linton, take your seat by *him*. He's not worth much, but I've nothing else to offer. I'm talking about Linton. Look at how she stares at me! It's strange how I wish to hurt people who are afraid of me.'

'I'm not afraid of you!' cried Cathy. She stepped close to him, and her black eyes were shining with anger. 'Give me that key!' She tried to seize it from his hand, and he was surprised by her boldness.

'Stand off, Catherine Linton!' he said. 'Or I shall knock you down.'

Cathy ignored this warning and attacked him with her teeth and fingernails. He dropped the key, then pulled her on to his knee and hit her again and again on both sides of her head.

I rushed to him, screaming, but he pushed me away. Then he let her go and she stood against the table, trembling and weeping. Linton was watching from a corner of the settle, as quiet as a mouse.

Heathcliff picked up the key, then went out to find our horses.

Our first thought was to find a way out, but all the doors were locked and the windows were too small to climb through. We were prisoners there.

'Mr Linton,' I said. 'You know what your father wants, and you will tell us. If you don't, I'll beat you like he does!'

'Yes, Linton,' cried Cathy, 'you must tell us.'

'Papa wants us to be married,' he said. 'He knows your papa won't let us marry now, but he's afraid I'll die if we wait. So we are to be married in the morning, and you will stay here all night. Then you can return home and take me with you.'

'The man is mad!' I said.

'Stay all night?' cried Cathy. 'No! I'll burn that door down, but I'll get out.'

Linton jumped up in alarm. 'Won't you have me and save me? Cathy, you can't go and leave me! You must obey my father, you *must*!'

'Be quiet!' she told him. 'You're in no danger, and I love papa more than you! The whole night! What would papa think? He'll be worried already.'

Just then, Heathcliff returned. 'Your horses have gone home,' he said.

*Cathy ignored this warning and attacked him with
her teeth and fingernails.*

'Mr Heathcliff, let me go home,' said Cathy. 'If I stay here tonight, papa will be miserable. And he is so ill. I promise to marry Linton. Why should you wish to force me to do what I'm willing to do myself?'

But he would not listen, and later we were taken to a room upstairs and locked in. At seven o'clock the next morning, Heathcliff came and took Cathy away. For the next four days, I was left alone. I saw nobody but Hareton, who brought me my meals.

16

On the fifth day, in the afternoon, the housekeeper came to my room and I was allowed to go downstairs. Linton was there.

'Where is Miss Cathy?' I said to him. 'Is she gone?'

'No, she's upstairs,' he said. 'She's not to go. We won't let her.'

'Take me to her!' I demanded.

'Papa will beat you if you try to see her,' he said. 'She is locked in her room. She's my wife, now, and it's shameful that she wishes to leave me. Papa says she hates me, and wants me to die so that she can have my money. But she shan't have it, and she shan't go home!'

'Have you forgotten how kind Cathy has been to you?' I said. 'And as for your money, she doesn't know you have any. Where is the key to her room?'

'I shan't tell *you* where it is!' he cried. 'It's our secret. Now, go away! You're making me tired.'

I decided it was best to leave that house without seeing Heathcliff or trying to rescue my young lady.

I arrived back at the Grange, and the servants were astonished and pleased to see me. I went straight to the master and found him very near to death.

'Cathy is coming, dear master!' I whispered. 'She is alive and well, and will be here tonight.'

Then I told him everything that had happened.

Four men were sent to fetch Miss Cathy from Wuthering Heights, but it was late that night before they returned with her.

'Ellen! Ellen!' she cried, throwing herself into my arms. 'Is papa still alive?'

'Yes, my angel, he is. Thank God you're safe, and with us again!'

She ran to his room, but I could not bear to be present at their meeting. I waited a quarter of an hour before going into the master's room. All was calm. Cathy's sorrow was as silent as her father's joy.

He kissed her cheek, then whispered, 'I am going to my Catherine . . . One day, my child, you will come to us . . .'

And then he died.

♦

Edgar Linton was buried beside his wife. The evening after the funeral, Cathy and I sat in the library at the Grange and talked. Cathy hoped to be allowed to stay at the Grange with Linton, and for me to remain there as housekeeper. But Heathcliff arrived even before we had finished speaking.

He walked straight in, like the master that he was (even though the Grange belonged to Linton now). Cathy jumped up, wanting to run from the room, but he caught her arm.

'Stop!' he said. 'No more running away! I've come to fetch you home.'

'Why not let Cathy stay here?' I begged. 'Send Linton to her. You hate them both, so you wouldn't miss them.'

'I'm looking for a tenant for the Grange,' he answered, 'and I want my children around me. Hurry and get ready, Cathy!'

While she was gone, he went across to a picture of Catherine Linton which hung on the wall. He looked at it for some minutes.

'Send that over tomorrow,' he told me.

Cathy came back and kissed me. 'Goodbye, Ellen,' she whispered. 'Don't forget to come and see me.'

'No!' said her new father. 'Do *not* come, Ellen Dean. When I wish to speak to you, I'll come here.'

I watched them both go.

17

I have been to Wuthering Heights once since that day, but I did not see Cathy. Joseph stood by the door and would not let me pass. But I have met the housekeeper, Zillah, in the village, and she has told me some of what happened.

When Cathy arrived at the farmhouse, she went straight to Linton's room and shut herself in. There she stayed until the next morning when she came down and asked Heathcliff to send for a doctor, because Linton was very ill.

'We know that,' he answered. 'But his life is not worth a penny, and I won't spend a penny on him.'

'But if nobody will help me, he'll die!' cried Cathy.

'I don't want to hear another word about him,' said Heathcliff.

Cathy almost made herself ill trying to nurse Linton alone. But one night she went to Zillah's room and said, 'Tell Mr Heathcliff that his son is dying.'

Heathcliff came to his son's bedside, where Cathy was sitting with her hands folded on her knees. He held a candle to Linton's face, and touched him. Linton was dead.

'Now, Cathy,' he said. 'How do you feel?'

'He's safe, and I'm free,' she answered.

Next day, Cathy told Zillah she was ill. She stayed upstairs in her room for two weeks. Heathcliff went up once to tell her that all of Linton's property – including Thrushcross Grange – was now his. She had no money, and no friends. Nobody else went to see her, except Zillah. The housekeeper went up twice a day to take Cathy what she needed.

One Sunday afternoon, Cathy came downstairs. She could not bear to stay in the cold bedroom any longer. She walked into the living-room like a princess. Hareton and Zillah were there, but Heathcliff was out. Zillah offered her a chair, but she would not take it. Hareton offered her a seat on the settle, near the fire, but she refused this, too.

Cathy got herself a chair and sat in it until she was warm. Then she began to look around. There were some books on a shelf, and she tried to reach them; but they were too high up and Hareton got up to help her. She didn't thank him, but he was pleased to be allowed to help her. When she began turning the pages of one of the books, he stood behind her and looked at the pictures. Slowly, his eyes moved from the pages of the book to her thick, silky hair. Without thinking, he put out a hand and touched it – as gently as if it were a bird.

She jumped round immediately. 'Get away, this moment!' she cried. 'How dare you touch me! I'll go upstairs again if you come near me.'

Hareton moved away, looking foolish. He did not speak a word for half an hour, then he whispered to Zillah, 'Will you ask her to read to us, Zillah? I would like to hear her, but don't say it was me who asked.'

'Mr Hareton wishes you would read to us, madam,' Zillah said immediately.

Cathy frowned, then looked up and answered, 'Please understand that I despise you, and will have nothing to say to any of you. When I wanted to see a kind face or hear a kind word, you never came near me.'

'But I asked Mr Heathcliff to let me —' began Hareton.

'Be silent! I'll go outside, or anywhere, rather than listen to you!' said Cathy.

Hareton became angry. 'You can go to hell!' he said.

After that day, Zillah told me, Cathy had no friend in that house.

MR LOCKWOOD'S STORY

2

Yesterday was bright and cold. I went to Wuthering Heights, and Ellen Dean, my housekeeper, asked me to take a letter to Cathy. Hareton Earnshaw was working in the garden when I reached the gate. It was locked.

'Is Mr Heathcliff home?' I asked.

'No,' he said. 'He'll be in at dinner-time.'

It was eleven o'clock. 'I'll wait,' I said.

He unlocked the gate and we went in together. Cathy was preparing vegetables for the meal. She seemed miserable and hardly looked up when we came in. I gave her the letter from Mrs Dean.

'What's this?' she said.

'It's a letter from your old friend, the housekeeper at the Grange,' I said.

Hareton seized the letter before she could open it. 'Mr Heathcliff should look at it first,' he said.

Cathy began to cry, silently. Hareton watched her for a moment or two, then threw the letter on the floor beside her. She took it quickly and began to read. After she finished reading it, she looked out of the window, across the moors.

'I should like to be riding Minny up there,' she said.

'Oh, I'm *tired*, Hareton!' And she sat back with a sigh, not caring or knowing whether we were there.

After several silent minutes, I said, 'My housekeeper never tires of talking about and praising you, Mrs Heathcliff. She will be disappointed if I return without news from you.'

She thought for a moment, then said, 'Does Ellen like you?'

'Yes, very well,' I replied.

'You must tell her that I cannot answer her letter because I have nothing to write with or on,' she said. 'Not even a book from which I could tear a page.'

'No books!' I exclaimed. 'How can you live without them?'

'Mr Heathcliff never reads, and he decided to destroy my books.' She looked at Hareton. 'But you have some of my books, don't you? You keep them secretly in your room, but they are of no use to you.'

Hareton's face became red. 'No, it's not true!' he said, embarrassed to have his secret discovered.

'Mr Hareton wants to learn,' I said, coming to his rescue. 'He wants to be as clever as you.'

'I hear him trying to spell and read to himself,' answered Cathy, laughing. 'I hear his silly mistakes! He's very funny!'

It seemed wrong to laugh at the young man for trying to improve himself, and I told her so.

'I don't wish to stop him,' she said. 'But he should not have taken my books of stories and poems. I cannot bear to hear him spoil them with his stupid mistakes!'

Hareton left the room, but came back soon after. He was carrying six or seven books in his hands and he threw them into Cathy's lap.

'Take them!' he shouted. 'I never want to read or think of them again!'

'I won't have them now!' cried Cathy. 'I shall think of you when I see them, and I shall hate them.' She opened one, and pretended to read it slowly and awkwardly, like a beginner.

Hareton became ashamed and angry, and he threw the books on to the fire. But I saw the pain in his face as he watched them burn, and I guessed the reasons behind his secret studies. He had hoped to win Cathy's approval, but he had only won her contempt.

Hareton went out of the room, and a moment later Heathcliff came in. He looked thinner, and there was a worried look on his face which I had not noticed before. When Cathy saw him, she immediately escaped to the kitchen, leaving the two of us alone.

'I heard you were not well, Mr Lockwood,' he said. 'I'm glad to see you out of doors again, partly for selfish reasons. It would be difficult to find another tenant for the Grange.'

'I am returning to London next week,' I told him. 'I've rented Thrushcross Grange for a year, but I shall not be living there any more.'

'Ah, you are tired of living in such a lonely place, are you?' he said. 'But if you're hoping to avoid paying me for the time you're not living there, then your journey has been wasted.'

'I'll pay you now!' I said, angered by his manner.

'No, no,' he replied coolly. 'I'm not in such a hurry. Sit down and take dinner with us. A guest that will not come back can usually be made welcome.'

The meal was a cheerless one, and I was not sorry to leave that unhappy house.

3

1802 . . .

Time has passed.

This September I went to visit a friend in the north. I was on my way there when I found myself within fifteen miles of Gimmerton, and I had a sudden wish to visit Thrushcross Grange. I was still its tenant, even though I had not lived there for some months. It was the middle of the day, and I decided I might as well spend the night under my own roof instead of at an inn. I could also go and see Heathcliff about my rent.

I reached the Grange before evening. An old woman came to the door.

'Is Mrs Dean here?' I asked.

'No, she doesn't live here now,' said the old woman. 'She lives up at the Heights.'

'Are you the housekeeper?' I asked.

'Yes,' she replied.

'Well, I am Mr Lockwood, the master. Is there a room for me to stay in tonight?'

The woman was very surprised, but quickly began to make things ready for me to sleep at the house.

Meantime, I walked across the moors to Wuthering Heights.

The sun disappeared, and by the time I reached the house there was a moon in the sky. The gate was not locked and I walked through the garden. Now there were flowers on each side of the path, and I noticed their sweet smell. 'Things *have* improved!' I thought.

Mrs Dean was sitting near the door. She was sewing, and singing a tune to herself. But she stopped singing when she saw me, and her face widened with surprise.

'Mr Lockwood!' she exclaimed. 'You should have told us you were coming!'

'I'm only staying one night, at the Grange,' I told her. 'But why are you living here?'

'Mr Heathcliff asked me to come after you went to London, and to stay here until you returned.'

'I want to see Heathcliff about my rent,' I said.

'Ah, you have not heard of Heathcliff's death, I see!' she said.

'Heathcliff, dead?' I said, astonished. 'Tell me what has happened since I left the Grange.'

We sat down, and Ellen Dean began the last part of her story.

ELLEN DEAN'S STORY

18

I was shocked when I saw Cathy. She had changed so much since her father died. Mr Heathcliff did not explain his reason for asking me to come to Wuthering Heights, but he told me to have the sitting-room and to keep Cathy with me. She seemed pleased about this, and I secretly brought her some books and other things from the Grange.

But Cathy soon became bored again. Heathcliff would not allow her to go on to the moors, and this made her sad. Whenever Hareton came into the kitchen, Cathy went out of the room or came to me. She would not talk to him. Then she suddenly changed her behaviour and began talking about him while he was in the room.

'He's just like a dog, isn't he, Ellen?' she said, scornfully. 'Or a cart-horse? He does his work, eats his food, and sleeps! What an empty mind he must have. Do you ever dream, Hareton? And if you do, what do you dream about?'

She looked at him but he would not speak to her.

'I know why Hareton never speaks when I'm in the kitchen,' she said another time. 'He's afraid I shall laugh at him. He began to teach himself to read once, Ellen. But because I laughed at him, he burned his books! Wasn't he a fool?'

'And weren't you naughty?' I said.

'Perhaps I was,' she went on, 'but I didn't expect him to be so silly. Hareton, if I give you a book now, will you take it? I'll try!'

She put one she had been reading into his hand. He threw it down.

'Leave me alone, or I'll break your neck!' he said.

'Well, I shall put it on the table,' she said. 'And now I'm going to bed.'

She whispered to me to watch whether or not he touched it, then went to her room. But Hareton did not go near the book.

I told Cathy the next day, and she looked sorry. After that, she often left a book where he could find it. Or she read aloud to me when he was in the room. But Hareton took no interest at all.

Then, in March, he had an accident with his gun and had to stay in the house. By this time, Mr Heathcliff no longer liked having people around him, and he would not have Hareton in his apartment. So Hareton spent his time in the kitchen, and this pleased Cathy.

One afternoon, I heard her say, 'I'm glad you're my cousin, Hareton.'

Hareton did not answer.

'Hareton! Do you hear me?' she said.

'Go to the devil!' he shouted.

'Cathy is sorry, Mr Hareton,' I said. 'And it would be good for you to have her as a friend.'

'A friend?' he cried. 'When she hates me, and does not think me good enough to wipe her shoes?'

'It's not I who hate you, it's you who hate me!' wept Cathy. 'You hate me more than Mr Heathcliff does.'

'That's a lie!' said Hareton. 'I've often made him angry by speaking up for you. But you still laugh at me, and despise me!'

'I didn't know you spoke up for me,' said Cathy. She stopped crying. 'Thank you, and I beg you to forgive me!'

She put out her hand, but he looked away and would not take it. Cathy hesitated, then she gave him a gentle kiss on the cheek. He kept his face hidden, looking at the ground.

Cathy fetched a handsome book and wrapped it in white paper. Then she tied it with ribbon, and wrote 'Mr Hareton Earnshaw' on the outside. She asked me to give it to him.

'And tell him, if he'll take it, I'll teach him to read it,' she said. 'And if he refuses it, I'll go upstairs and never trouble him again.'

I did as she asked. After hesitating some time, Hareton unwrapped the book.

Cathy went to sit beside her cousin. He was trembling, and all his rudeness and anger had melted away. A few moments later, I saw two happy faces bent over the pages of the book.

19

The next day, I came downstairs to find Hareton and Cathy in the garden. She had persuaded him to clear some fruit trees from a large piece of ground, and they were planning to bring plants from the Grange.

I looked at the ground in horror. The fruit trees were Joseph's favourites, and Cathy had decided to have her flower garden in the middle of them.

'Joseph will complain to the master when he sees this,' I exclaimed. 'What will you say?'

'I forgot they were Joseph's trees,' said Hareton, 'but I'll tell him I did it.'

When Heathcliff heard about the trees, he asked Hareton why he pulled them up. But it was Cathy who answered him.

'We wanted to plant some flowers there,' she said. 'I told him to do it.'

'And who gave *you* permission to touch anything about this place?' demanded Heathcliff, very surprised. 'And who ordered *you* to obey her?' he asked Hareton.

'You shouldn't mind if I have a few yards of earth,' said Cathy, 'when you've taken all my land!'

'*Your* land? You never had any land!' said Heathcliff.

'And my money,' she continued, returning his angry look.

'Silence!' he shouted. He stood up, his face white and full of hate. 'Get out of here!'

'If you hit me, Hareton will hit you!' she said. 'He'll soon hate you, as I do.'

'Don't speak to him like that,' Hareton whispered to her. 'Come away.'

But it was too late. Heathcliff had his hand in her hair. Hareton begged him to let her go, but Heathcliff seemed ready to tear Cathy to pieces. I was just getting ready to go to her rescue, when the master dropped his hand from her head and on to her arm. He stared at her face – then put a hand over his eyes. After a moment, he said, 'You must learn not to make me angry, or I really shall murder you one day! Now, go with Mrs Dean and stay with her. And if I see Hareton talking with you, I shall send him away. Your love will make him a beggar. Now, leave me, all of you!'

He went out and did not return until the evening. While he was away, I heard Hareton talking with Cathy. He did not want to hear about the bad things from Heathcliff's past, he told her.

'I won't hear a word against him, even if he's the devil!' said Hareton. 'How would you like *me* to speak badly about your father?'

And then Cathy understood: Hareton had become fond of Heathcliff after all those years.

I went to sit with them, and they got a book and began to read. They were still reading when Heathcliff returned. He looked at them, then picked up the book and looked at that. Then he put it down and signalled for Cathy to leave the room. Hareton went after her. I was going to do the same, but Heathcliff stopped me.

'It's a poor end, isn't it, Ellen?' he said about the scene he had just observed. 'I work to destroy the two families, using all my strength; and when everything is ready, and in my power, I find I can no longer enjoy their destruction. And I'm too lazy to destroy for nothing. Ellen, there is a strange change coming, and I'm in its shadow at present. I take so little interest in my life that I hardly remember to eat and drink.'

'Are you ill?' I asked.

'No, I'm not.'

'Then you're not afraid of death?'

'Afraid? No!' he replied. 'I have neither a fear nor hope of death. Why should I? I'm healthy, and will probably live to be an old man. And yet, I cannot continue in this condition! I desire only one thing – to be with *her*.'

♦

After that evening, Mr Heathcliff stopped meeting us at meals and ate only once a day. One night, after the family were in bed, I heard him go out. It was the next morning before he returned.

'Will you have some breakfast?' I asked him.

'I'm not hungry,' he said. He was pale and he trembled, and his breathing was fast.

At dinner-time, he sat down to eat with us. I gave him a plate full of food, and he picked up his knife and fork. Suddenly he put them down again and turned eagerly to the window. Then he got up and went out. We saw him walking up and down the garden as we ate our meal. Hareton thought we had upset him, and went outside to ask.

'Is he coming in?' Cathy asked, when her cousin returned.

'No,' said Hareton, 'but he's not angry. He seems happy about something.'

After an hour or two, he came back inside. There was a strange smile on his face.

'Have you heard good news, Mr Heathcliff?' I asked.

'Where should I hear good news?' he said.

'Tell me why you are so strange,' I said. 'And where were you last night?'

'Last night, I was on the edge of hell,' he said. 'Today, I am within sight of my heaven.'

He did not go out again and, at eight o'clock, I took a candle and his supper to him. He was beside the open window, but not looking out. His face was turned towards the dark room. The fire had gone out and the room was filled with the damp evening air.

'Shall I close the window?' I asked him.

The candle-light fell on his face – and I was filled with horror. Those deep, black eyes! That smile, and terrible paleness. It was the face of a ghost, a devil! In my terror, I let the candle go out.

'Yes, close it,' he replied, in his familiar voice. 'And bring another light, quickly.'

I hurried out and found Joseph.

'The master wants you to take him a light and make up the fire,' I said to him. I could not go back into that room again.

The candle-light fell on his face — and I was filled with horror.
It was the face of a ghost, a devil!

Joseph went in, but came out again. He explained that the master was going to bed. We heard him climb the stairs – not to his own bedroom, but to Catherine's old room.

'Is he a ghost, or devil?' I thought. And then I reminded myself how I had looked after him when he was a child, and watched him grow up. How silly it was to imagine such horrors!

♦

He was late coming down to breakfast the next morning, and would eat nothing. He stared at the opposite wall, looking up and down it. His eyes were bright with excitement.

'Are we by ourselves, Ellen?' he asked.

'Of course,' I said, for the others had gone out before he came down.

Now I realized he was not looking at the wall, but at something closer to him. Whatever it was, it seemed to give him both pleasure and pain. The imagined object seemed to be moving, and his eyes followed it eagerly.

He ate none of his breakfast, but went out soon afterwards.

That evening, I did not go to bed until late, and I could not sleep. Heathcliff returned after midnight. He did not go to his room, but stayed downstairs. I heard him walking up and down, hour after hour, and talking to himself.

I could understand only one word that he spoke . . .

'*Catherine.*'

Each time he spoke it, it was followed by some wild sound of great suffering. At last, I went down to him.

'Is it morning, Ellen?' he said. 'Come in with your light.'

'It's four o'clock,' I answered.

'It's not my fault I cannot eat or drink,' he said.

As soon as he heard the others getting up, he went off to his room. But in the afternoon, when Joseph and Hareton were at their work, he came to the kitchen.

'Come and sit with me!' he demanded, with a wild look at me.

I was frightened, and refused.

He turned to Cathy. 'Will *you* come? I'll not hurt you. No! To you I've made myself worse than the devil! Well, by God, there's *one* who won't refuse me! She never leaves me alone! It's too much to bear!'

He went out of the room and did not come back again. Through all of that night, and far into the morning, we heard him talking and weeping to himself.

Hareton wanted to go to him, but I told him to fetch the doctor. The doctor came, but Heathcliff refused to see him, saying he was better and wanted to be left alone. So the doctor went away again.

The following evening was very wet, and it rained all through the night. Next day, when I took my morning walk around the house, I saw that the master's window was open, and that the rain was pouring in.

'He cannot be in bed,' I thought. 'He must be either up or out.'

I found another key to his room, and went to see.

Mr Heathcliff was lying on his bed. His eyes met mine, and they were bright and fierce. I was frightened, and jumped back. Then he seemed to smile. I could not believe that he was dead, but his face and throat were washed with rain. The bedclothes were wet, and he was perfectly still. I touched him, and he was cold. I could doubt no more: he was dead!

I closed the window, then combed his long black hair. I tried to close his eyes, but they would not shut. They seemed to be laughing at me, and I was afraid. I called Joseph.

'The devil has carried off his soul!' said Joseph. 'How wicked he looks, laughing at death!'

Heathcliff was buried next to Catherine, as he had wished. Hareton watched with tears running down his face . . .

♦

I hope he has slept peacefully since that day . . .

There are those who say that they have seen Heathcliff and Catherine walking on the moors, or near the church, or even within this house. It is all nonsense, yet I don't like being out in the dark now. And I don't like being left alone in this house. I cannot help it, and I shall be glad when they leave it and go back to the Grange.

MR LOCKWOOD'S STORY

4

'Hareton and Cathy are going to Thrushcross Grange then?' I said, as Mrs Dean finished her story.

'Yes,' she said. 'As soon as they are married, and that will be on New Year's Day.'

'And who will live at Wuthering Heights?' I asked.

'Joseph,' she said.

'And any ghosts who choose to live here,' I said.

'No, Mr Lockwood,' said Ellen, shaking her head. 'I believe the dead are at peace.'

At that moment, the garden gate opened. Hareton and Cathy were coming back from their walk. They stopped to take a last look at the moon . . . and at each other. I did not wait to meet them, but said goodbye to Ellen and hurried away.

I walked home through the churchyard and found the three gravestones on the slope next to the moor. Catherine's – the middle one – was half-covered with **heather**. Edgar's had grass growing on it. Heathcliff's was still bare.

*I walked home through the churchyard and found the three
gravestones on the slope next to the moor.*

I stood there in the moonlight, among the flowers and heather, listening to the soft wind breathing through the grass. I wondered how anyone could imagine unquiet sleep for the sleepers in that quiet earth.

EXERCISES

Vocabulary Work

Look back at the 'Dictionary Words' in this story. Make sure that you know the meaning of each word.

1 Look at these words.

   a Which *five* of them are words for PLACES?

   scoundrel   courtyard   idiot   housekeeper
   moors   vicar   churchyard   heir
   tenant   stables   fireplace

   Write a short description of each place, saying what it might look like or be used for.

   b The other six words are all words for ... what? Write short definitions of these words to show their meanings clearly. You cannot use your dictionary to help you – look back at the words in the text instead.

2 What part of speech are these four words: nouns? adjectives? verbs?
   bless, weep, thrust, haunt

   Write sentences with the words in them, to show their meanings clearly.

3 Write three more sentences with the words in these groups, to show their meanings clearly.

   a heather/churchyard/headstone

   b housekeeper/shelf/settle (noun)

   c treatment/sullen/scornful

Comprehension

Mr Lockwood's story (part 1)

1 What do you think the word 'wuthering' means?

2 Why is it a suitable name for the house where Heathcliff lives?

Ellen Dean's story (parts 1–5)

3 Why was Hindley jealous of Heathcliff when they were children?

4 Heathcliff comes to Thrushcross Grange to see Catherine. Where does Ellen first see him?

Ellen Dean's story (parts 6–10)

5 Who in these chapters says . . .?

a 'I love him more than you loved Edgar. And he might love me, if you would let him!'

b 'Oh Cathy! Oh, my life! How can I bear it?'

Ellen Dean's story (parts 11–17)

6 Put these events in the right order:

a Edgar brings Linton to Thrushcross Grange.

b Cathy and Ellen are locked in a room at Wuthering Heights.

c A letter arrives from Edgar saying that Isabella is dead.

Mr Lockwood's story (part 3)

7 When Mr Lockwood arrives at Wuthering Heights, he doesn't know Heathcliff is dead. But two changes tell him that things have improved since his last visit. What are they?

Ellen Dean's story (parts 18–19)

8 Who is Heathcliff talking about when he says: 'She never leaves me alone!' at the end of the story?

Discussion

1 Which do you think was Heathcliff's strongest motive for wanting to own Wuthering Heights and Thrushcross Grange – ambition or revenge?

2 Do you believe in ghosts? Why do you?/Why don't you?

Writing

1 a You are Isabella and you have just met Heathcliff. Write a letter (150 words) to a friend describing this exciting man and how you have become attracted to him. Remember, you know nothing bad about him yet.

b You have now been married to Heathcliff for two months and have learned how cruel and heartless he can be. Write a letter (150 words) to the same friend describing what you have discovered about him and how you feel now.

2 Look at the picture of Wuthering Heights on page 6. You have been asked to try and sell this house for the owners. Write the advertisement for the newspapers. Try to make it sound as attractive as possible (about 50 words).

Review

1 Write a short review of this book (200 words) for other students. How will you describe it? A tragic love story? A ghost story?

2 Why (even if you *didn't* like this story) do you think this book has remained popular for nearly 150 years?